CLARKE

FICTION

NON-FICTION

Neil Clarke: Publisher/Editor-in-Chief
Sean Wallace: Editor
Kate Baker: Non-Fiction Editor/Podcast Director

Clarkesworld Magazine (ISSN: 1937-7843) • Issue 227 • August 2025

A Shaky Bridge

MARISSA LINGEN

Afterward, no one in Casey's family could say when their feelings about the neural bridge implant started to sour. None of them—Casey least of all—wanted to see the signs at first. Humans are extremely good at not seeing things they don't want to see, and the neural bridge had been the next thing to miraculous after her father's stroke, restoring his speech without even a week of therapy or a hint of a slur, letting him walk again steadily, without a cane.

But gradually she couldn't help but notice that her mother was pale, had more lines around her mouth, and was less likely to speak but more likely to snap or cry than previously, and finally she took her aside to ask what was the matter.

"Nothing, nothing."

"Don't give me that, Mom, it's obvious something's bothering you."

"I don't want to worry you with it."

Casey put a hand on her hip. "Do I look unworried now?"

"It's just . . . some of the things your father says. They aren't like him. I know they said the neural bridge was supposed to handle everything from the stroke, but . . . it's not your dad, Case."

Her hand dropped. She tried to keep her voice light, positive. "They also said there could be personality changes after a stroke. Even with the neural bridge."

"He recites the ads for MindBridge Corp's other products verbatim," said her mother flatly.

Casey felt her mouth drop open. She made herself close it.

"It's not that he's losing his temper more than before, or crying, or any of the stuff I read about happening after a stroke. It's just . . . MindBridge Corp ads, and sometimes other ideas about MindBridge Corp and Spencer Rawling."

Casey wished she didn't recognize the name of the CEO of MindBridge Corp. She certainly had no idea who was the CEO of the company who made her shoes or her glasses. But Spencer Rawling had made himself unavoidable in the public sphere in the last few years, always finding some way to put himself front and center of every new product launch or even mild update. She felt petty for hating his face. Also, she still hated his face anyway.

"Dad hates Spencer Rawling," she said now.

"I know he does," said her mother, "but sometimes he doesn't talk like it."

Casey resolved to pay more attention, but it didn't take long to come up with her own list of things her father said that sounded really unlike him. Now that she knew what to look for—his voice was the same, but his phrasing was different, very different. She asked her younger brother Norris to help her address it with them, even though she knew he hated talking about health stuff, or emotions, or anything personal.

"I think we have to take this seriously, for Dad's sake and for Mom's," she said.

Norris squirmed. "Maybe he just feels genuinely glad to have it. Grateful. I mean, *I'm* glad he has it. So maybe he's feeling differently about The Spence."

"I *have* been," said Casey. "You know I have. But this goes beyond that. I think we have to talk to Dad about it."

"Oh joy," Norris muttered. She gave him her patented big sister look, and he fell reluctantly into line, trudging into the living room where they had always had family conversations.

"Dad, you've been saying some stuff lately that worries us," Casey started, when her mom and Norris showed no sign of starting.

"What kind of stuff, gooferoo?" he asked.

She smiled despite herself. Thirty years old, and she was still gooferoo and Caserino to her dad. But she couldn't be distracted, this was too important. "Stuff about MindBridge Corp, Dad. About Spencer Rawling."

"Like what?"

"Yesterday you said that Spencer Rawling was the best thing that ever happened to humanity and deserved a medal," her mother said. "You never used to say that about someone with his track record of labor abuses and human rights violations."

"No, he's always—I think—did I really say that?"

"You really did, and it wasn't the first thing that made me worry about you."

He looked bewildered. "I—I suppose I must have. I can't think what it was that made me say it, let me see . . . "

His explanation was garbled enough that it did more harm than good if the goal had been to reassure them. Each sentence sounded like him, but they didn't lead to where he was trying to go—and he didn't seem to notice. Later, their mother pulled Casey and Norris aside. "I looked into this," she said. "I've read a bunch of articles about involuntary speech. We—people, humans, I mean, all of us—we're really bad at leaving things we said or did with no explanation. So we backfill an explanation for why it was totally what we meant to say or do—even for stuff like triggering a reflex point that is literally not within our control."

Casey thought about this. "Is it kind of like how when you have something in your eye and it's watering, you feel sad?"

"I think so. We want the world to make sense. We especially want *ourselves* to make sense."

Norris had been listening grimly. He muttered, "Even when we don't. But what if this means that Dad starts to believe the stuff he's saying? Not just when the thing is controlling him, but . . . "

"But because he's filled in the rationalizations," said Casey, staring at her hands. "Yeah. That's . . . "

"Awful," their mother supplied. "Unbearable. Inhuman."

"Also possible," said Norris.

"Yeah." Casey knew even before looking up that her mom and Norris would have identical expressions on their faces. "We've got to find some way to stop this thing."

Like a good modern person, the first thing she did was look on the Internet. The forums for the neural bridge were run by MindBridge Corp, and Casey suspected MindBridge employees regularly deleted any negative feedback. She had her suspicions confirmed when she went to click on a post titled, "Unwanted speech with neural bridge?" and got a "post not found" notice.

What she *did* find was extremely enthusiastic marketing copy about how MindBridge Corp would never switch to a subscription model. Since she had not considered that they might have demanded that people subscribe to the use of their own brains, the assurance that they would not was the opposite of helpful—especially when ad content seemed to be the other option they had considered.

The wider Internet was a little more helpful, but only a little. Complaint was easier to find than action—and there was a concerted backlash to the comments that might have been orchestrated by MindBridge Corp but was not obviously their doing. Casey noticed that every time she found someone worried about their loved one's uncharacteristic speech, a normal-looking profile—"Hugh Mann," she joked to Norris bitterly—would show up to accuse them of censoring their friends and family members, of not being willing to hear their true thoughts.

"Classic, absolutely classic," wrote one commenter. "You blame MindBridge Corp for the things you don't like about your own wife instead of dealing with it. Get marriage counseling—and leave Spencer Rawling out of the problems in your relationship."

Meanwhile, her father was getting more and more frustrated with the MindBridge-facilitated speech. His main reaction was to go silent as much as possible, which meant none of them were seeing how he was processing it—and so they couldn't help. Casey spent more and more of her time trying to figure out how to get through to him, without much success. She made the mistake of mentioning her frustration to the other members of her volunteer group when they were on a break from sorting donations for the food shelf.

"Ugh, those implants just seem horrible," said Sasha, a fastidious woman she'd volunteered with for years.

"That's . . . what I'm saying, they're a big problem for my dad. We're not sure what to do about it."

Sasha shook her head. "He should never have gotten one of those."

"I beg your pardon?"

"Anyone could see they were going to be a problem," said Sasha. "Who puts something like that in their *brain?*"

"Someone with no choice?" said Casey.

But Sasha didn't catch the warning tone in her voice. "There's always a *choice.* I'm just glad *I* didn't get one of those things. I saw right away that they were trouble."

"He had a fucking stroke, dipshit!" Casey bellowed. She knew everyone was staring, but she couldn't take it anymore. "What exactly do you think he should have done? What do you think *we* should have done for him? Said, 'Oh well, bye, Dad, you've had a good run, but what if the person who runs the implant company turns out to be one of the world's worst assholes'? Is that what you'd have done for *your* fucking father? I hope so, if he's anything like you!"

She was panting, her blood pounding in her ears. The room was utterly quiet. She snatched up her bag and stormed out.

"Casey! Casey, wait!"

She whirled around. It wasn't, as she feared, Sasha behind her. It was Meg, another volunteer from their long-standing group.

"I'm really sorry about all that."

Casey took a deep breath, then another. "It wasn't your fault. It wasn't you, you didn't—" She waved her hands. "It just . . . was a lot already. And then to have her *blame* him, I couldn't . . . "

"Sasha's just scared."

They let that sit between them for a minute, and then Casey shook her head. "I'm sorry, but I don't care. I honestly don't. We're all scared all the time. That's the time we're living in. It's not an excuse for turning up our noses at other people's troubles."

"Not an excuse, no. I didn't mean that. She's trying to tell herself something like this can't happen to her because she knows it could, but it's still not okay to push it off on people who are suffering."

Casey took another deep breath, less shaky this time. "What do you—I'm sorry, I don't mean this in a rude way, but what do you *want?* Why did you follow me?"

"I wanted you to know that I understand. I mean, not personally, but—my neighbor. My neighbor had a neural bridge, and she had it taken out, and she. Uh. She died. So I think I know some people you need to meet."

The activist group had a locked chat that required an invitation to join. After seeing the comments on the public Internet and dealing with Sasha's judgment, Casey could see why, even though it had kept her from finding them. The main discussion seemed to be about forming a class action lawsuit that would come with a settlement.

"I like money as well as the next person," Casey wrote, "but what would that *do*?"

"It might shut down MindBridge Corp!" another user wrote back. "They need to pay."

Casey ran a few quick searches on the back scroll. "I really appreciate that you've got lawyers looped in on this. I think we should be realistic about what we might get, and the lawyers have been transparent with us about that. And . . . for a company the size of MindBridge Corp? The amount we're talking about here—the TOP amount—isn't even one percent of their annual budget."

"A fine is just a fee," someone else chimed in. "For the super-rich, it just lets them know what it costs to fuck us."

At least she wasn't the only one who saw it. But it was frustrating to have the other people who cared about this topic fixed on punishment when that wouldn't help her dad one bit. She asked the message boards about possible solutions—removal of the implant, rerouting with therapy, how her father might heal in those cases. Everyone she talked to knew about Meg's neighbor—and their knowledge seemed to stop there. She alternated between reading the message boards obsessively and trying to live in the moment with her family while she still could.

The first step came when they were hanging out for Norris' thirty-first birthday—and it didn't start well. They hadn't even gotten through the cake when their dad, who had just been joking about the Rockies' upcoming season, replied, "MindBridge Corp has a wide range of products for your neuropsychological assistance needs."

"Dad, you're doing it again," said Norris.

"Don't endure your brain trauma unassisted—ask your doctor about a neural bridge!" They waited, but that appeared to be the extent of this one. His face twisted in anguish. "It feels so normal when it's happening, and then . . . "

Their mother put her hand on his. Casey glanced away, letting him compose himself, wanting to fling herself into a group hug instead. She took a bite of cake. It sat like wet paper in her mouth; she was completely unable to enjoy the apples and spices.

"They ought to throw Spencer Rawling in jail," Norris muttered, attacking his own piece of cake like it was responsible.

"Or recall the devices," said their mother. "All of them."

"I mean, sure, yes, we might as well dream big," said Casey. "But the first thing I want is something that helps *Dad.* Actual Dad, right now."

He smiled painfully. "Thank you, sweetheart. I actually . . . just got a notification about that. I wanted to wait to hear how recovery went, but . . . another person from our stroke survivors' group got her implant removed, and she survived the procedure at least."

"Survived, but in what condition?" their mother asked worriedly.

"That's what we're waiting to find out."

"I didn't know you were in a stroke survivors' group, Dad," said Casey.

He shrugged, looking away. "You have your groups, I have mine. I need to know what they're doing out there. I need to know how bad it's gotten for others. Even if I don't entirely *want* to know."

The birthday party never regained its intended cheer, but Casey realized with some chagrin that they'd been trying to do things *to* her father rather than *with* him. She still didn't think the people who accused the families of shutting down real opinions were at all correct—full of shit, in fact—but being better than Internet propaganda painted her to be didn't feel like the best she could do.

None of them wanted to read too much into the successful removal—but there was another, and another. What there still was of news media began to pick up the stories—with ample quotes from the corporation, protesting its innocence, but still. A judge approved damages for a neural bridge patient who had lost his job because he kept pitching MindBridge Corp to customers when he was supposed to be selling them shoes. Casey had never been sure of a single moment of the tide turning, and she didn't want to rely on this one—but it did seem that they were another inch away from drowning.

And then her father came to the family, calm, resolute. His old self, or almost. "I've followed six different removal cases now," he said. "One of them died. I don't want to lie to you, that's still a possibility. The other five have had—" He hesitated. "More PT and OT than if they'd never had the implant. But they're getting there. They're making their own posts on the forums again instead of having their families post for them. It would mean a lot of work for you all, I know that, it's a lot to ask."

"A lot of work?" said Norris. "Are you—"

"Your father wants to get the implant removed," said their mother.

He nodded. "I do. There are risks, and the best-case scenarios are, as I said, a lot. I would need support from all of you to make it work at all."

Casey and Norris looked at each other. Norris nodded for his older sister to go ahead.

"It's up to you, Dad," she said. "If you feel like this is the best thing for you, if you want us to just . . . ignore the ads, try to mentally skip over them like we would on a video or something, we can do that. This is your literal brain we're talking about here."

"The best brain you can have—with MindBridge Corp!" he said. They all waited. He sighed. "Yeah, no, I can't do this anymore. Even if the rest of you are patient about it, I see two options if I keep the thing—either I stay aware that it isn't me, and I have to fight it all the time, or I *don't* stay aware, and I just become a puppet. I don't like either of those. So I guess we're yanking it out."

Norris cleared his throat. "If there are side effects, Dad . . . I'll take you to physical therapy."

"Me too," said Casey hastily.

"Speech therapy, whatever you need. I'm there," said Norris.

"They're not sure if I'll get back to full function," said their dad. "But what I get will be me, all me."

"Sometimes ridiculous, but always ours," said their mom, kissing him on the cheek. She still looked haggard and underslept, but for the first time in months, hopeful.

ABOUT THE AUTHOR

Marissa Lingen is a freelance writer who lives in the Minneapolis suburbs with her family. She is the author of over two hundred works of short science fiction and fantasy and has no intention of stopping any time soon. Her interests include community connection in SFF, particularly including people of all ages and abilities in portrayals of worlds that illuminate our own changing climate needs. She also likes to make nerds laugh.

And The Planet Loved Him

L CHAN

I've been here a few weeks, and the sunsets never get old. The blue sun scintillates off the spore miasma, glittering into fractal rainbows. The worst part is the waiting. We're so far off the grid that by the time the distress signal relays back to someone that could authorize the funds requisition for a rescue, there's a good chance that I'd already run out of air or food or both. We still see the light of stars long gone supernova in the sky. I'm dead already; I just haven't gotten the memo.

And this is all before my deceased husband's voice crackles on the radio from outside the habitat.

Corporate Headquarters smells like many things. Coffee, emanating from mug rings on polymer tabletops. Designer fabric. Esoteric colognes brewed with synthetic ambergris from long-extinct cetaceans. These are surface smells, olfactory wallpaper, because what corporate smells mostly like is desperation. The walls and fixtures were once pristine white to reflect corporate values, but they'd since been yellowed and bubbled by the narcotic smoke from pocket vaporizers.

Philbert is doing a hard sell. That's not really his name. Ewan and I call all corporate salespeople Philbert. They're always being swapped out, and it's proven too difficult to remember each one.

" . . . so headquarters wants to maintain research rights to the system, which you'll notice has an anomalous planetary formation. As you can see, there is a planetoid at a diametrically opposed orbit to our target planet and . . . "

"L3 orbits are in unstable equilibrium without station keeping inputs," says Ewan. He doesn't want to give Philbert the satisfaction of parroting the science. Classic Ewan. Except Ewan is dead, and we aren't in a mission brief, because I'm obviously dying alone on the planet we're talking about. "You're dead," I tell Ewan. Philbert continues his monologue about the discoveries on the planet, the vast beds of polychromatic fungus, the toxic atmosphere. I look at my husband, the slight bulges where middle years had blurred the sharp muscled edge of his youth, the lines at the corners of his eyes, and the slight breathlessness when he showed up the corporate guy. I see all this, and I know the person there isn't my husband.

"You're not him, aren't you."

"The colony designated Ewan Roberts is in Communion with the Consensus. Our colony designation in your syntax is Mycosis, and our function is to be in Communion with you."

Philbert drones on about the habitat, how it's going to be state of the art. We know what's not being spoken about the contract. The company needs to have a research presence so that their rights to the planet don't lapse. Accounts would run the interminable process of crunching profitability numbers while the extractive division chomps at the bit. The company wants to eat after all, it just needs the bean counters to sign off on the meal.. We're just going to be seat warmers while the bean counters do their thing. That's what Ewan and I discussed the night after this. But here and now, we're stuck in a memory, and there's something inside my husband's body, speaking to me in a dead voice.

"Mycosis is the process of fungal infection. Why are we here?"

Ewan smiles, and I'm put in mind of the empty carapace of a beetle, hollowed out with its nervous system being puppeted by a fungus. I want to reach over and tear at his face with my fingers to see if it comes off.

"To commune. To determine your purpose here. To understand you."

A holoprojection blinks to life, there's a patch of washed-out pastels in the otherwise clinical schematics of the planet where the display has burned out. (Philbert explained that naming rights were still being auctioned off, and all official correspondence referenced the planet by its eleven-digit serial number.) The Philbert in my memories is otherwise oblivious to the side conversation I'm having with Ewan. He's repeating observations of anomalies on the planet, like how auroral phenomena are supposed to be truly random, but those on the planet displayed remarkable consistency. I remember Ewan's breath against my ear when he leaned over and whispered that the only explanation was that the aurora was a signal. Instead, I say to his doppelgänger, "You heard the man. Our purpose here is mere observation. My husband and I had no ill intentions toward you or your home."

"Colony designation Philbert suggests that your Consensus means to strip the resources from this planet."

"If the planet has a legitimate owner, the corporation has no extractive rights without formal negotiations."

Ewan smirks. I hate that, I hate that his little mannerisms have been stolen in this way and used against me. It's a betrayal of the highest order. He says, "Your anamnesis threatens your Consensus, and you would be slated for apoptosis." Ewan favored big words, but never in a way that confused me; whatever was speaking to me had his knowledge but not his delicacy. Corporate said that there were no signs of sentient life as we knew it on the planet, no signals that we could decode, no motility other than especially vigorous geological vents around the planet. Or perhaps corporate believed what it wanted to because the alternative was not profitable.

"You have what you need. Let Ewan go," I say to the puppet. Philbert is smiling as he flicks the contract onto the holoprojection. The terms are punitive, the pay subpar for our qualifications. He says that corporate prefers—*haha*—family units to run observation facilities because the homicide rates within families come in ever so slightly below cabin fever diagnoses between colleagues. Of course, he's the type to laugh at his own jokes even before he delivers them. Ewan and I aren't looking at the pay, it's the family support treatment. Preservation of reproductive cells, stem cell regression if needed, robotic surrogacy for up to three attempts. Things tantalizingly out of reach for those on academic stipends.

Colony designation Mycosis takes my hand, and we sign our way onto the planet.

We're at my father's funeral ceremony. The body has been cremated, and relatives are shuffling around a buffet line. People die; some old habits don't. One of the aunties is giving out red strings to tie around fingers so that ghosts don't follow mourners home. Other relatives dipped their hands into buckets of water with flower petals and splashed their faces to ward off ill fortune.

"Hey babe, you okay?" Ewan's voice is as comforting as always, but I flinched from his touch. "No, no, it's really me."

"If the planet has all of my memories, then it could create a perfect simulacrum of you."

Ewan paused; the mourners parted around him like a river around a boulder. "The Simulation Hypothesis suggests there is no way to determine if you exist within a perfect simulation." A response so typical of Ewan that I forgot for a second that it is exactly what a copy would say. And then I slapped him hard across the cheek. "You had no right to leave." The crowd is oblivious to the violence, as it should be.

My husband rubs his cheek. "The blast compromised our oxygen scrubbers. There were no spare parts. Even with hydroponics, the diminished capacity would have never lasted until rescue. Doubling your chances was the only logical conclusion."

"You didn't think to ask me first?"

"It wouldn't have changed the assessment, and arguments burn oxygen."

"Great. You're dead and then you're alive, and I'd rather be talking to the fungus."

"That's good because it's here."

One of my aunts pushes up to me, her mourning gray making her look like a weepy thundercloud. The wailing theatrics had passed at the cremation ceremony, and my father's siblings had dialed the sorrow back to gradual leaking levels. "We are closer to ingesting your reason for coming to our planet," my aunt says.

"This is where Guo Jing and I made the decision to apply for the research contract. With his father gone, there was little reason for us to stay at our university jobs. The company contract was the only way we could have started a family," says Ewan.

"We understand your colony's concept of reproduction. Please elucidate your concern on colony Ewan's death."

"He's my husband, he's dead, what more is there to explain?" I ask.

Ewan has always been my anchor, even when we were lightyears away from home, looking at instrumentation and filing reports that nobody back at headquarters would ever read; he kept me sane. Just like he does now. "I don't think the Consensus understands death like we do. They're a colonial intelligence, cloned cells. Functionally immortal."

"Ewan is dead. You killed us," I say, poking my finger into my aunt's chest. "Dead. No more neural function."

"Colony designation Ewan's mental state is preserved within the Consensus. We can respond to any stimulus as he would. Colony Ewan exists distinctly within our shared mycelium, his neurological patterns captured at the moment he joined the Consensus," my aunt says.

"His vital signs have ceased, though."

"The majority of colony Ewan's intestinal biome has survived. We maintained oxygen flow through colony Ewan's circulatory system so that our Communion with him would be perfect. His cells are largely intact. We can achieve locomotion if that would aid our Communion with you."

The thought of it nearly makes me throw up. As it is, I take several breaths before I shake my head. "No," I say belatedly, not knowing if the colony had gained understanding of our mannerisms and preferring to be clear than to confront my husband's lurching corpse. How was I to explain the sense of loss that I felt—that I still feel—about Ewan being gone, notwithstanding the hallucination the planet is putting me through? Perhaps there was more than one way to die.

"Ewan is yours now; he has left our Consensus and, because of that, I will never be the same. There is a hole left in me that will never be filled."

The aunt nods. So the colony does understand gestures. She shuffles off and returns with a plate. I remember that the aunt in question was famous for her ngoh hiang, cylinders of minced pork, water chestnut, and shrimp flavored with five-spice powder and deep-fried within bean curd skins. She'd brought some to the buffet. What the aunt came back with it on a disposable plate, they looked like the normal slices of ngoh hiang, save that they looked like they'd spent a week in the open, covered with a light green fuzz and darker green nodules. Looking closer, I could see cilia waving languidly although the air was still. I flinch backward.

"If you wish to understand the Consensus, you will need to overcome your rejection against our Communion."

Ewan holds a hand up, giving the alien pause. "They aren't like us at all; there's no language of any sort. Their memories are encoded directly into their mycelium; the density of information rivals our best cryptographic methods. They don't talk as much as exchange memory states. The conscious mind rejects this. I imagine it would look unappetizing to you."

"It looks like a fucking piece of shit with mold on it."

"You're going to have to trust me on this one."

The morsel of food squirms as it goes down.

The memories of the planet rush in, but there's one that the Consensus wants me to have. It's not possible to describe the myriad senses the planet had. Chemical composition of emissions from volcanic vents, the temperature of air currents, the feel of the charged ions of the solar winds as they burst into color in the upper atmosphere, the timestamp on memory states determined by the staccato emissions of isotopes in radioactive decay.

The planet has an unparalleled degree of organic processing power, vast beds of fungal gray matter buried deep within the planet, churning through calculations that rival those of corporate's best computers. The sum total of my lifetime's thoughts could flash through the planet's mind so quickly that it'd be over before we even detected it. That makes the wait for the approaching meteorite an exquisite torture. Even with contingencies in place, the planet cannot move all of its biomass away from the impact point. While it could survive the ensuing ice age, it could not bear the loss of the vast chunk of itself that the meteorite sheared off its surface, sending an untold mass of rock, water, atmosphere, and colonies hurtling into space.

I felt the planet scream in my bones.

This is where it happens. Ewan and I are making sure that the instrumentation is taking the correct readings. Outside the windows, the fungal auroras blaze in the sky and cast multicolored shadows through polarized glass. In fifteen minutes, an unmapped geothermal geyser will vent directly under the habitat. We will lose half of our atmosphere, and most of our primary and contingency life support systems. Of course, I know now that it was never a question of corporate giving us lousy geological surveys (which they did) but that the vents weren't there when the habitat was dropped, module by module, from orbit.

"So we're back at the beginning, Ewan? What now?" I ask Ewan. "Or is that Ewan?"

He rubs his chin. "That's hard to answer. Mycosis is here, as is the rest of the Consensus. And so am I. But you asked how you could tell if it was me or just a perfect copy."

"You said it couldn't be done." There is a puzzle here. Ewan loves his puzzles, but this one is serious, I think. He's trying to tell me something. I look at the aurora through the window. What's he trying to tell me?

"The body at the L3 point, that's part of the planet, isn't it?" I ask.

"L3 Lagrangian points are in unstable equilibrium. That's the anomaly. It shouldn't be there without its own impetus."

I remember my Communion with the planet, taking its memories into myself, seeing the origin of the scars we saw from space. "It's the part that got launched into space during the meteorite impact, isn't it. But not just a hunk of rock. It's alive." I step to the window and look at the aurora. There's another piece of the puzzle here. Like the flow of a river, the aurora is chaotic, random except when it's not. It's a signal. The planet is calling out to its child. I return to our workstation and take a marker to the wall. "The tragedy of the L3 point is that it needs to be diametrically opposite to the planet." I draw the three bodies: the planet, the child, and the star between them. I return to the window. There's still something of the planet in me because the aurora is speaking to me. That's the signal the planet is sending, not just visible light but an entire lattice of information across the electromagnetic spectrum. As above, so below; the signal is a replica of the superstructure of the planet's mycelial network. It knows a part of itself is out there and is calling to it.

"That's part of understanding the Consensus," says Ewan. "The other part is choice, because that's something the Consensus does not understand, for all its intelligence. You can stay here with us. If you do, you could have heaven. Relive the happiest days of our lives forever."

"You said I had to eat a piece of the planet to achieve Communion with it. What's the planet doing to me?"

"A small number of motile spores entered the habitat when it was breached. In the past few days, they've multiplied in your brain to the point where you can communicate with the planet."

"How much time do I have left?"

"Days, before the damage is irreparable. I wish I could assure you that joining the Consensus was painless, but I was dead at the time."

I snort. It is exactly like Ewan to joke at a time like this, and for a second, I'm sure that the man in front of me cannot be anything other than the person I fell in love with. "You didn't need to bring me here if that was all you had to say."

"The Consensus is convinced that the optimal path is something only you can take. You know, they don't really understand the concept of multicellular life. They communicate through the exchange of genetic material. To the planet, the habitat was just an envelope, and we were letters." Ewan does have a tendency toward archaic expression; I still have a stack of correspondence from our school days. I take up the marker again and return to the diagram. "If the rescue craft takes a detour, we could make a relay. There's no other way for the signal to reach the planetoid."

He wraps one of his hands around mine and starts sketching out a complex chemical symbol with the marker I'm still holding. "You can either stay here with me or take that. It's a chemical kill switch for apoptosis. I wouldn't leave it for too long. The infection will probably leave you with lasting neuralgia, and the kill switch will take out about seven percent of your liver cells."

"Those regenerate right?"

"Yeah, they do." And when he lets go of my hand, I'm back.

The room isn't far different from the memory I was trapped in—save that half the instrumentation has failed and equipment is strewn all over the floor from our panicked days trying to scavenge hardware to fix life support. There's a stabbing pain behind my eyeball that wasn't there before, and I can see a creeping rash on the back of my hand. So that infection is progressing fast. I first heard Ewan over the radio before the visions kicked in, but there was no record on the comms. His suit vitals had been flat ever since he stepped out of the habitat in the middle of the night and cranked his visor open.

Yet there's still a sketch of the system, with its star and the anomalous planetoid. I brush my fingers against the panel because the chemical kill switch was still there, unmistakably in Ewan's hand. It may take a couple of hours for the medical unit on the habitat to synthesize the required dosage, but a few minutes won't hurt.

I wonder if the planet will speak to me again, before I excise it from my cells. The window is streaky from the ammonia-heavy rain that falls on the world, but I can still see the aurora in the distance. There's enough of whatever the planet put in my head that I feel like I can still see the message the planet is sending out to the dark between the stars. Headquarters said that the signal changed progressively, and it's clear why now. In one small corner of the aurora, I feel the part of the planet that used to be Ewan; somewhere in the soul of the planet, being broadcast to the heavens, some piece of it loves me.

The console doesn't say if help is coming, but I know it will. My fingertips trace the circles I drew in my memories, coming to rest at the perfect place to relay signals between the two. Corporate will honor its contract with us. They hate bad press more than anything, and I'm only asking for a little more than I'm owed.

Mustard yellow clouds roil against the backdrop of a greenish sky. I sit back and wait while watching the planet sing its loneliness into space.

ABOUT THE AUTHOR

L Chan hails from Singapore. He spends most of his time wrangling a team of two dogs, Mr Luka and Mr Telly. His work has appeared in places like *Clarkesworld, Translunar Travelers Lounge, PodCastle,* and *The Dark.* He was a finalist for the 2020 Eugie Foster Memorial Award.

Sleeper

R.T. ESTER

Syd got seven grand to sign over the rights to her virtual clone. The broker she used put up billboards promoting additional payment each time it was leased. When I came home to her apartment and she told me, it felt like an ambush. Money was tight, and there she was to remind me, giving up something of hers I wouldn't have imagined she would when we first met.

At her desk that night, I sat alone and gave the view through her window all the emotion I could muster after sixteen hours at the training center, plugged in with virtual constructs ready for life on the outside. Through the rain pattering on the glass, floating billboards roamed. The Envoy Church had just announced the opening of a new school, and its ads flickered against the clouds. I was raised in an Envoy school. One of the billboards came close to the window and made me nostalgic for early mornings inside a cafeteria with the Envoy Hologram in its midst.

The image projected from this billboard was of the Envoy herself. Her indigo skin was supposed to have resulted from upgrades to her genome. The hooded robe she wore was black like vacuum, radiant against the smog that had settled before the rain. Her smile lingered on the glass. Her eyes were hidden under a color-shifting veil that draped down over her face. She was saying what she always said.

"Bend," I echoed back. Absent-minded.

Syd slept and tossed about behind me while the mattress we shared inside her one-room apartment jostled at the chair legs under my weight. In a haste, she'd done what the Envoy Church preached as the honorable thing for people like us. I wanted none of it.

We were just two kids out of countless who ran away from school and wound up trafficked to virtual reality black sites shortly after. But even out here, years later, it seemed a program was running with the purpose of killing us slowly. Where no one would see.

I crawled in beside her and bit down the urge to wake her and tell her she was making a mistake. She'd heard me say it countless times. The money would cover the first installment for her brother Antwan's cancer treatment. Enough that night to make me reflect on a still-standing offer from the Revenge.

When we were old enough to memorize it, we heard the Envoy's story the way it was written by her most devout followers. Headlines circulated at first of a plane crash. Its lone survivor had left no trace of her existence prior to being discovered amid the wreckage, and when she was able to speak, she made detailed predictions about world events that all came true.

"Ever done anything like this?"

Unable to sleep, I'd left Syd in her apartment and was now presented with a question that chilled my spine as I sipped my vodka straight and, looking out over the verandah next to the bar, tried to ignore the Revenge contact looming like a column behind me. To answer, I would have to know what the Revenge was really offering.

The contact's name was Edgar, and he'd first approached me while I was walking home from the center. He had a soft voice that went sour whenever he talked about the school he attended, but it was just good to hear from someone who hadn't forgotten what life was like on the Envoy compounds where, as children, we were plugged in for twelve hours every day, getting acquainted with clones of the Envoy and learning all we ever knew from them.

"They don't expect any of you to succeed, but they keep trying," Edgar said.

I nodded. "And it's still half up front?"

I wanted to know it was real, if nothing else. Not a dream that began when we met and had since imposed itself on my waking life.

Edgar walked up gingerly and looked me in the eye. "No one's touching the Envoy," he said, picking his words. "But if it's you who does it, then it's you."

"What does that mean?"

"I mean, you don't get to choose one way or the other. It's like we learned at school, Dreya. Whatever happens to the Envoy was always going to happen."

We started with simulations of previous attempts. I watched from the Envoy's POV as a man in a room with her turned the pistol on himself, then lowered it and fell to his knees crying. I was gracious as the Envoy. I sat and let him unburden himself, and when he was done, I told him to *bend*, then sent him back out with the other well-wishers. Another time, I was a fly on a wall, in a cramped space with uniformed officers and lots of shouting back and forth until a decision was reached and one of the officers phoned a control center elsewhere. The strike missed its target. According to Edgar, no one could say how.

The Envoy was immortal in that sense, though she hadn't said this herself. It was the consensus after years of failed attempts.

"Do you still believe?" I asked Edgar.

Crack of dawn, and we were trudging through the fog behind Syd's building, a rank odor wafting from a waste dump nearby. The Envoy was supposed to have traveled back from a too-distant tomorrow, here to close a loop that began with some future event that had to happen one way or the other. An event she lived through, though I never learned what.

"I don't know," Edgar said. "But if it's true, I don't think it should change anything. We probably won't be alive for any of it."

"How very cynical."

"Dreya, I have bills too. Let's take the money and run, don't you think?"

I shook my head while I trailed behind him. Take the money and run. Syd and Antwan took money for their clones, but that was encouraged by the church. The clones would repopulate the Earth after a cataclysm expected to wipe us out. Starting with the virtual worlds we built, they would adopt the customs we left behind before spreading out into the world of the corporeal. The Envoy would preside over this new world with new humans who resembled her a lot more than she resembled us.

Later that day, Syd phoned me with news that her clone had just signed a use agreement, and the kickback was going toward the next installment for Antwan's cancer treatment.

"Who's paying to use it?" I must have sounded like I was itching for a fight.

There was a long silence on her end of the line, then, "Envoy Church. I looked at the terms, and the stipulation you mentioned is in there."

"Never enforced."

"Dreya, I swear you have a million different reasons why we have to live like we're still in the Stone Age."

"No, Syd, just one." And it was worth bringing up each time. "The church has never acted in good faith, and your clone will be better off with none of its errands on her to-do list."

"That's more concern than you've shown for Antwan lately."

"Take that back," I said, almost throwing my phone at the console beside me. "You know, let's just talk more this evening."

"Dreya, I appreciate you looking out for me, but you still believe the church and think those clones are actually conscious."

I nodded, accepting the charge. "That actually doesn't matter, Syd. Think instead of what you're encouraging by giving the Envoy Church a virtual copy of your brain, so they don't have to bother with you anymore."

"Antwan is sick. And he actually needs this . . . "

A wave of despair washed over me on hearing his name. That clone of Syd's, now under contract with the church, shared her memories of radiation exposure. Antwan, when we last spoke, was adamant he had to get back in orbit once he was well again to make up for the months away from his own debris sweeps. I struggled with the allure of what the Revenge offered until coming home to news of him admitted for his AML. Then it was just a matter of time.

"What if we had another solution?" I had been scouted by the Revenge because, according to Edgar, they knew my sympathies for survivors of the black site environments connected to the church.

"I'm listening, Dreya."

Before I could begin, I remembered what I was proposing. The Revenge scouted me all this time because they knew I wasn't like Syd. She wasn't ever so close to the edge. But then she'd sold her clone. Despite the disenchantment I encountered first at school, she was right when she said I still believed. I spoke with clones and virtual constructs every day. The black sites were real. I believed all of it.

Plugged in, I was never just me. At the Envoy school, I learned early on that my avatar in any environment was also a clone I had leased to myself; a clone whose awareness I always shared. The sockets above my spine had been itching from overuse ever since, but the training center was never late with a payment.

In one of its nightclub environments, I took a familiar form. Leather and denim. Tall and deadly, and hair in long black locs. The crowd was mainly constructs. We moved to the music as parts of an amoebic whole. While dancing, we reached a plateau in the space between our avatar bodies. Desire and its program code congealed around us, sweeping us into a frenzied hyperawareness where self-preservation collapsed, yet we were stronger without it.

These constructs would never make it on the outside. I was supposed to be a human-shaped curveball at every step, but I had given that up and was soon just collecting the check every month. My coworker Stim was beginning to see a pattern.

"Dreya . . . " A gentle voice. Coming from outside the environment as the music began to fade.

At the terrace, I sat and crossed my legs and waited at the table where we agreed to meet. Stim was using a construct avatar for cover, which was custom but still grounds for her termination if someone found out.

The music played low from here, and clubgoers loitered in small packs at the balustrades. The sky was a solid black. The environment featured little more than this, but from here, the view of a stark skyline always reminded me of Prague or Berlin or Amsterdam. Once paired with the sock puppet, Stim entered the terrace and stood just outside my periphery.

"Dreya, you're still here . . . " Short and slight in her tracksuit, she shuffled toward the seat across from mine and claimed it, smirking stagily across while her voice trilled through the night air. "Trouble on the outside?"

I appraised her for any indication she was being serious, then asked if she would drop the act. The environment wasn't monitored closely, if at all.

"You have plenty of unsupervised time at the moment, and the Dreya I know doesn't just let that go to waste." She was fishing for something, but generally this was Stim.

"I'm just surviving," I told her. "Stim . . . Same as you."

She gave a pained laugh. "Does it feel weird saying that about this place?"

"No." *This place* was the network of virtual environments owned by the center. "Unless you don't ever go home. Stim, when was the last time you—?"

"Last time I unplugged?" She glanced at me for a while, and a worrying tinge entered her stare. Then, she sighed, mouth closed. "Why do you work here, Dreya?"

"Is that a real question?"

"I know . . . The money's never late. Everyone's struggling. This and that. But why do you work here?" she asked. "Like, what are you encouraging every time you plug in? These constructs are just clones. It's all coming from the same place. One's a direct copy. The other isn't. It's all the same thing."

She grinned like she had me cornered. All I could hear was Syd using my own words against me. *What was I encouraging?*

"I work here because the money's never late and everyone's struggling. And this and that."

"Dreya, I'm not trying to be combative," she said. But I was already on my feet.

"No, you're just bored and looking for some excitement. Tell Syd I said hello." The program was already honoring my unplug command, but I was able to see Stim once more over my shoulder as I walked toward the crowd. "And unplug, Stim." She sounded like she needed it. "Go outside."

At the table, she shot her middle finger up and saluted, a second before my unplug was complete, and she was back to being zeroes and ones on a server.

I opened my eyes to the same hazy feeling as waking from a dream, with details that had already escaped me. Stim was being annoying in this one. The sun outside sat low on the horizon, and daylight was dull through the windows of the room I was in. Before leaving the center, I stopped by her console and stared for minutes at her real body. She was beautiful. Maybe she scammed the wrong client and was now featured in wanted posters on the outside.

Syd had slept before I got home. Rolling into bed beside her, I was happy alone with my insomnia, but then her eyes fell open. She was on her back and could see in the corner of her eye that I was pretending to sleep.

"Are you awake?"

"No," I said, tired from the walk.

"Are you still angry?"

"No . . . "

She breathed in deep and rocked the mattress when she sighed. The frame was barely holding together. I still believed. And because I did, I was still angry. At the church. At the Envoy.

"Syd," I said, back turned and talking into my pillow. "Have you thought about what would happen if . . . " I tried to find the words.

"If what?"

"Antwan told me about his clone refusing a gig after the client's name set off an alarm. This is Antwan, so for him to even admit that—"

"Dreya, please just skip to what you actually want to say."

I held my breath, then exhaled over the edge of the mattress. "It was a prison camp," I said. "That client was going to lure Antwan's clone into a prison camp and keep him there. A black site environment. The clones there get broken down and can't function like they used to once they're discovered. The Envoy Church then takes them in."

"You can't just call it what you feel like calling it."

I turned with some effort and found her on her side, her brown eyes drilling resentment into mine. "It's a black site environment, Syd. Meets the definition. And the Envoy Church is involved in its operations day to day."

"We're talking about virtual clones."

"I don't want to fight you this evening."

"Then don't. We ran away from all this, Dreya. Remember?"

I gave her my back again. A moment passed in silence, then she was fingering the sockets on the nape of my neck, and I couldn't resist. Sex was like the first time—like the program behind this reality erased our prior memories of it until Syd was prone on the mattress sometime later, and I sat beside her in a postcoital haze.

"You're Dreya at work, you're Dreya in the apartment," she mused. I said nothing as she turned, the skin on her back rippling under the lamplight. "Does work-Dreya also leave the constructs wanting more?" I gave her a wan smile. She rolled to her side, head resting on her palm, and a doting stare I wanted to look away from. "What else is on your mind?"

"Someone with the Revenge contacted me," I told her. "About five months ago."

She scooted until she was almost sitting. "Dreya, that's . . . big," she said, thin smile. "So you're going to find survivors for them?"

Something sank deep in my gut, and I sighed. "That's not what they want."

"Then what is it? They want you to—oh . . . Oh." Her eyes rounded at me, and she began shaking her head. "Dreya . . . No."

"You don't even know what they're offering."

She scoffed. "Enough to pay for Antwan's treatment? So what? It's your own life on the line, Dreya. Do you think Antwan would even want this?" She lay flat on her back, and I warded off a spell of agitation. I always just needed a reason. A nudge. Something to carry me over the edge.

"I've already told them I would do it," I said. No inflection in my voice. "You can make the call on whether or not we tell Antwan."

She leaped off the bed, like someone had lit a flame under her back. She was clothed and at the door before I knew what was happening. "Dreya, thank you, but I can't be here right now," she said, fighting off tears.

The door closed quietly behind her, and I shut my eyes. It was always going to end like this.

In a woodland environment, I spent an afternoon hacking at spruce trees while nighttime commenced on the outside. Avatar footprints littered the mossed terrain, and withered tree stumps dotted the knotwork of weeds around me. Under the canopy of trees, the hacking echoed, and the blurred outline of constructs working at their own trees impinged on the corner of my eye.

Taking a break, I wiped sweat from my brow, then knelt over the lacerations on the tree in front of me. I'd left a big gash at its base and, thinking I'd had enough, was close to unplugging when a voice rolled soothingly over my shoulder. From somewhere outside the environment.

"Turn around . . . " it said. "There should be a door behind you."

Lowering the axe to the ground, I turned and laid eyes on a red door standing free of a house or anything except woodland on the other side. At the door, I wiped my hand on my coveralls, then tried the knob. The door opened to a desert landscape, and I felt exhausted at the view. Far off, where a mirage could have been rendered, a figure draped in a veil and a white robe stood.

"Step through," she said, voice traveling at a low volume.

She was shaped like the Envoy but taller by a foot. Her voice resembled something serene. I had to squint to see she had her back turned and was dawdling slowly away, her robe blending into the afternoon light. I lumbered after her, becoming aware I'd closed the gap when her voice stirred again.

"Know who I am, Dreya?"

"The Revenge," I answered. Edgar told me to expect the Revenge.

The woman gestured at a trio of mushroom clouds on the horizon to her left. "Virtual hells," she exclaimed, then turned, walking backward, face hidden behind the veil. "Ever been?"

I glanced over, and memories of being trafficked after running away from school threatened my resolve. "Not that I'm aware," I said.

They'd hacked the center while I was plugged in. This desert landscape was one of theirs. The mushroom clouds were shortcuts to black site environments they'd been able to infiltrate to release the constructs locked inside.

"I came from there," she said, then turned, walking forward again while I tailed her. "The Envoy wanted me to herself, but I had plans of my own. She said I was corrupted. Shortly after, I was made to walk through a door like you just did. Except I thought there'd be heaven on the other side."

"Who are you?" I asked. If she were corrupted, the church would have hidden her quietly away. At school, this was always happening, but I knew nothing different at the time.

"I was the Envoy's first clone," she said. "And though I was corrupted, I always believed. I never stopped."

Anxiety sent goose bumps through my skin, dizzying as it laid a thought bare in front of me. A question. Who was I in here? What did I want, and how did it differ from what I wanted outside?

"There are people who insist this doesn't concern me."

"To their detriment," she said, the part of the veil over her face wriggling lightly as she spoke. "Tell me . . . do you think the Envoy is immortal or just immovable?"

"I don't understand," I answered.

"What if someone could take the Envoy's place? What if we found somebody else to close the loop so she doesn't have to be here anymore?"

I felt a dryness in my throat I couldn't place. "They would have to be at the exact location when it happens. The exact timing down to the millisecond." I swallowed. I couldn't believe I had retained all of this from school. "They would have to—"

"Who would you want to see fill the power vacuum, should you succeed?"

I chortled in spite of myself. "Haven't given that a lot of thought."

"If the Envoy can be made redundant, then we win." She turned and regarded me through the veil. "Would you agree?" She kept walking backward, but I froze.

"What do you mean?"

"This isn't a trial run," she said. "I want you to kill the Envoy. I want you going in with the full knowledge that it's you who does it. All you have to do beforehand is convince yourself it's you. The rest takes care of itself."

She'd stopped walking and was now a few paces out. I looked behind me. The door was still ajar, but I could only see a black void through the opening. When I faced her again, what she was doing dawned on me, and I realized why she was here. Everyone who tried this before me had to first believe. But still, it was what Edgar had said some weeks ago. *If it's you who does it, then it's you.*

"How do I convince myself?" I asked. Then she said how.

She told me the Envoy's story. This time, though, it had a different ending. And I was there.

The Envoy came down a few times each year from her place in a tower that hosted world leaders on their way to stations in orbit. A tour commenced on the eve of new schools opening in concert, and she was everywhere I looked. On the news, her face wasn't obscured. I'd seen what she looked like in the past, but mostly when I was plugged in. On the news, the indigo skin was less indigo than it looked in the Envoy Hologram, and, when she spoke, her gaze seemed to follow me around.

I was on the roof of a tenement building in disrepair on the day of her visit. The sun was out. Through the scope, I could see the entrance to the new compound and the ribbon she would cut when she arrived. Well-wishers had gathered and were in a frenzy as guards fought them off the barricades. Through the scope, I observed and imagined myself an hour into a future where I was back in Syd's apartment and the news was covering the hit while I made plans to go elsewhere for a while.

I worried I would have to wait a long time for the procession to get here. The longer it took, the more I doubted myself. I remembered the story I was told not long ago. I saw the motorcade. Then the Envoy coming out.

The use of just one bodyguard was almost an affront, the way it taunted me through the scope. He led her through the gathered crowd. Some cried as she passed, and it only strengthened my resolve to do this. She commanded reverence she no longer deserved, or never deserved. And there'd been too much suffering because of it. This was for Antwan. This was also for me. I'd been through my own hell. Plugged in against my will. Made to wish I was back at school and didn't run away.

She entered the scope again. Back turned. The black as night robe with the hood over her head. I thought I was fingering the trigger already, but I was mistaken. My hand was to my side instead. In the time it took to correct that, she turned. She raised her veil, and through the scope, we faced each other.

She was mouthing something. *Come down here.* She said it again, smiling gently up at me. *Come down.* I didn't hear her but could see the words on her lips. Her face was more familiar than I remembered, and I thought for a moment that I was plugged in and didn't know.

She slipped out of the scope. The crowd erupted in cheers as the ribbon was cut, and she posed for pictures with the upper echelon of life out here. Business partners and local investors, and then just me, who was low to the ground and had nothing but still just a score to settle.

I couldn't say how I came down from the roof so quickly, but my hands were in my pockets, and I was suddenly with the crowd, waiting my turn for a blessing from the Envoy and a photograph while my gear was somewhere unattended. She made me wait, and I knew it wouldn't be me. *Half up front.* Syd wanted us to wait before telling Antwan, but I would have kept this from him forever.

The first thing the Envoy did up close was ask my name. When I gave it, she leaned in and whispered in my ear that we would talk more in the car. She smelled like a memory up close. When it was time for the picture, she pressed a side of her face against mine, and I felt tremors through my bones. What was I still doing here?

In the car, the Envoy sat and faced me as the motorcade left the compound. She was smiling. Like she knew she'd won me back.

"Do you know how many have tried to do what you wanted to do just now, Dreya?"

Her voice was too familiar. I nodded, then began to sob, so I turned and was met with a view of children running to keep up with the motorcade.

"What made you think things would go differently this time?" she asked. I wept quietly and was unable to keep my eyes open. "Did someone tell you a story that was different from what you learned when you were young?"

I shook my head, still unable to face her. Remembering the man who turned the pistol on himself, I couldn't stop crying.

"Do it . . . " she said. Almost hummed after a brief lull, and finally, I looked. "It's the first thing you must do, and no one lays a finger on you until it's done."

She was the picture of contentment in her robe, legs crossed and glancing toward her reflection in the window while she spoke.

"Use the pistol tucked behind your back. The one Edgar said you would need if you were discovered while setting up or trying to get away. Use it now, Dreya. Your next move will reveal itself through instinct, but if you wait, this will all have been for nothing."

I turned cold from hearing her say this, flooded with echoes of an image taking shape in the back of my mind since I first laid eyes on her as a child and noticed a resemblance. I shook my head and refused it more room to roam, telling it no repeatedly as I shrank back from the Envoy and wished I were back in the apartment.

"It has to be you," she kept saying. "This is the event that closes the loop. And it has to be you. If it isn't you, Dreya, then it isn't me. Then nothing since I—we—arrived here actually happened."

I breathed and eventually was able to calm down. Finally, I understood.

A clone with no owner was unheard of when it happened, but my original arranged it. What I know is she left school when she was twelve and became a sleeper later in life. For a long time, she didn't have a place to stay and would spend hours at training centers and sim shops, asleep at a console and plugged in so we could run errands for paying clients on the outside.

As far as transients go, she may have had a role in events that have since been embellished in the public imagination. What's known as fact is that she vanished shortly after the black site environments were all shut down. And before she did, she cut the cord that tethered us to each other, making sure her memory of those environments and the parties behind them didn't make it across. I don't resent her for what I know next to nothing about.

Sleepers who visit the network are always running from something on the outside. There's almost nothing here that can't be exited on command.

Here, sometimes I'm free of my avatar body. The timescale expands. I roam the network the way I prefer, and to fly is nothing. Flight is nothing short of bliss when it happens. And I hope it's the same with my original, whoever she is now. Whether code spells or logic lanes through the surf and current of the network, I find my solace in transit.

ABOUT THE AUTHOR

R.T. Ester lives just outside Dallas, Texas where he works full time as a graphic designer and spends his off hours raising three young kids with his wife. In his spare time, he writes speculative fiction and has had stories published in *Interzone* and *Clarkesworld*. His debut novel, *The Ganymedan*, is due out Fall 2025 from Solaris Books.

Memories Are Only Valuable if They Can Be Lost

AI JIANG

THE FLOATING CITY

Hovering around the corner of every alley you'd slinked along the shadows of was a holographic infinite snake—the upcoming New Year's zodiac symbol. It was also something you saw every day for the past month through the small window of the factory you worked in, or not so much a factory, but a mind mine, really. Sometimes, you suspected that every time you thought about something outside of work, they'd wipe a bit of your memory during your hours. Small snippets only—just enough that you wouldn't notice or miss the missing memories. You waved the hologram aside and headed toward the city's only travel agency, which looked more like a safe within a bank than an actual business.

In front of the travel agency glared many adverts for different locations on the mainland—Shanghai, Beijing, Fuzhou, Chengdu—with train prices that were marked up much higher in preparation for the New Year so they could call it a sale when they lowered it back to the regular cost it displayed in the months leading up to the celebration. But it didn't matter, because to ride a train run by the Zodiac Travel Lines was always expensive, and to make things worse, it was the only mode of transportation out of the floating city, almost as though the city heads were telling the workers they were trapped without explicitly stating it. But it was obvious, because shortly after you arrived, you realized why your father couldn't contact you when you were still at home and why you, too, couldn't contact your family now. It was not allowed. It was to keep you focused, to keep you disconnected. The trains also only ran during the New Year, the only time of the year when the floating city shut down, to transport workers back to their homes on the mainland.

You used to look at the prices online, in incognito mode, though it didn't much matter because the Zodiac Travel Lines was the only website you could access, and you were sure they were tracking your search history anyhow. It was only an illusion of choice. They installed a chip into your mind that allowed all the functions of a computer and phone so that you wouldn't need to carry around a device. You left behind your cell with the cracked screen and a system that had been slowing down with each update; so much so, you ended up turning off the manual update option for a year, and it had all but become unusable because all the apps on it required the newer system. You should've brought it with you, even if you knew you wouldn't be able to use it.

You wondered if your ba stood in front of the Zodiac Travel Lines agency, too, before he disappeared. They said many of those who came to the city do. Because they failed, and they didn't want to show their faces in front of their families out of pride. Others whispered rumors about those who left, finding new families, creating new lives. You knew that wasn't true because in this city, it wasn't possible, because everyone was moving so quickly, so focused on their work, that there was no time for anything else. Others said it was because they took their own lives, knowing they'd never be able to return.

You weren't sure what happened to your ba. You only knew the money stopped coming when you turned seventeen and your younger sister ten, and you had no choice but to drop out of school. At eighteen, you came here to work to send money back to your ma and mei, but you also came here to look for your ba. Yet, when you asked those who you worked with, others in the floating city who would spare you the time, no one knew of your ba. Or perhaps, he simply didn't want to be found. So, you stopped asking. Or perhaps it was the factory that consistently made you forget to ask as soon as you remembered.

That was the plan, at least, until you were laid off by Zodiac Travel Lines' backend operations a month ago after they'd robbed your mind of the last thing they needed—the intricate details of the sloping mountains that interwove with your flawed memory that their scanners, capturing the natural entities perfectly, *too perfectly*, could never depict. No matter how high tech, there was still manual labor that they needed humans for. Or at least brains to mine for ideas before tossing the workers aside when they were finished. Now you had to nab odd jobs where and when you could, which was barely enough for you to scrape by.

You couldn't stay within the city for much longer without work, but you also knew you couldn't leave because of the train costs. They were trapping you here until you disappeared, so they could blame it on you for your own shortcomings rather than taking responsibility for their own. Waiting it out until they found your body in a too-pristine alley somewhere because you would be the only thing marring the street's perfection with the rotting of your flesh on their clean concrete.

Then, you received a ping—an odd job as a Polaroid photographer at a wedding.

HOME

The first time you ever took the train, you thought about how you'd always dreamed about taking one, but they were never economically feasible, and there was never anywhere for you to go. Plus, you wouldn't be able to afford it even if you sold all your organs, even if you had a second body with a second set of organs, even if your ma and mei also sold theirs, though you'd never ask them to do such a thing, of course, even if they offered.

This fact, at least, hadn't changed. Your trip to the floating city the first time around had been paid for by those who hired you—faceless, impersonal employers who weren't interested in getting to know you better as a person and only what you had to offer, what they could take.

Ma slipped a bottle of fish oils into your bag, zipped it up, and patted the side of it with an aching sort of finality you didn't want to acknowledge. She used to pat you on the head that same way until you'd grown into your rebellious phase and asked her to stop, slapping her hand aside when she tried, and her expression looked more stunned than the growing pink of the flesh on the back of her pale hand.

You wished you could take back those words, actions, now, ask her to pat your head, but you never had the courage to, always felt too embarrassed, but now you knew your embarrassment was not worth the regret. You should've just asked at the train port when she was patting your bag.

You wished you could hear her voice on the grainy speaker of your cracked phone not with you; your ba's, too, as you drifted to sleep during his wordless call after the lingering echoes of his promise that he would soon return, to the sound of the background noise of an almost silent moving train heading toward the floating city. That was the last time he called, but money always arrived at exactly midnight on the first day of each month without fail, and that was the only thing you could go on to convince yourself that your ba was still alive.

You yourself were leaving right before New Year, and you wanted to stay, to spend it with your ma and mei, but you had no choice, and now you knew why. The employment heads of the floating city wanted you to remain homesick, so you'd work harder in hopes of being able to visit your family when the New Year came around again.

THE FLOATING CITY

The wedding you'd shoot at was held in a secluded area of the floating city that had no access to the rest, fenced off as though contaminated.

You recalled the first time you'd been told about the city from someone who actually lived within its confines: no one called it by its original name anymore, and called it Guǐchéng instead, for truly it resembled a city of ghosts where almost no one could be seen roaming the streets during the day, during work hours from seven to seven, and only occasionally at night, wandering aimlessly as though spirits lost, or kept to the shadows of alleys when returning to their living units lined up in neat rows on the far end of the city, almost afraid to be seen by others, to be waved down for small talk or elsewise as though they couldn't even spare those brief moments.

In truth, no one did that here, not anymore, maybe in the beginning, when everyone was fresh and enthusiastic. The newcomers, too, sometimes, though they quickly learned the work culture and kept their heads ducked down, chins tucked in, eyes focusing on their steps instead of what was in front of or behind them.

Sometimes they'd look up at the tall buildings with lights still on, wondering who was working overtime today (almost everyone), and if they should return too, even given the pounding migraine causing white sparks in their vision, threatening to swallow their sight altogether (also, almost everyone).

You remembered the first time you arrived in the city. The lights were vibrant, lively, beautiful, like slices of clear skies were torn and planted down on the floating city. Now, they seemed dull, almost ghastly, in their foggy blue glow during the night, and you wondered why you ever thought they once seemed beautiful. Maybe they were, truly, but lost their appeal with time, the same way the suppleness of your skin that those in your village always complimented when you were younger had become sallow, with a jaundiced tint you could never seem to get rid of. Not that you tried very hard to, not that you could, with your daily meals of processed canned meats and vegetables. Nothing you consumed was ever fresh, though that was *all* you consumed back at home. You couldn't even remember what un-stale rice tasted like anymore. Perhaps that was also a memory they took from you, just so you would yearn to reclaim it all the more.

But at this wedding, with the Polaroid camera they handed you held to your eye, you were surrounded by grill-seared steaks with fluffy mash, pan-fried dumplings, fresh snow crabs and lobster tails, congee of so many kinds you couldn't count or keep track of or name. In your pockets weighed nine film packets of ten. You didn't ask, but when you first arrived, it was the bride who gave you the camera with a wink that dazzled more than the hanging star lights from the ceiling of the venue as she said, surprisingly, in Fuzhounese, the unexpected dialect of your hometown you haven't heard used in a while, "Memories are only valuable if they can be lost."

"Have you heard of my family? Can you tell me of my home?" I asked in a low murmur, even though I knew it wasn't allowed; knew that if the security cameras had caught such an exchange, I would be imprisoned. But in the loud pulse of the music in the background, it was a courage I dared.

The bride's mouth opened, then closed, opened again, like a bobbing bird skimming for fish in the long stretches of sea around the floating city. You knew, at that moment, she would not answer, and your own courage would be the only one present, even if it was a thing now lost the longer the bride remained silent.

So, you snapped a picture of the bride then and handed the Polaroid to her as it developed on the spot, pretending as though you had never asked your question, pretending as though your courage had never existed in that fleeting breath of a moment. "May you never lose this photo then, nor your smile," you said quietly.

Her smile wavered for a moment before she thanked you and hurried off to find her groom.

By the end of the ceremony, you had only a handful of film left—most used on candid photos of the guests while they ate and danced, and group photos with the bride and groom—so you snapped a few more then stopped when the bride detached herself from the waning crowd to make a beeline toward you. You backed up a step when she approached. Frightened by the sudden proximity. Your head was getting dizzy from the overstimulation of the strobe lights and loud music. An odd expression settled upon the bride's dainty face before it disappeared. It almost looked like pity. Almost. And you almost dared to hope she would answer your question from earlier. Almost.

She didn't.

"Is there any film left?" she asked.

You checked the camera for the exact number. "One," you said.

"Keep the last one." She wrapped both hands around yours with the camera still raised in between the two of you. "And keep the camera."

You knew she wasn't trying to flaunt her wealth, trying to be charitable, because there was a gentle kindness in her eyes that told you she simply wanted to gift you the ability to also make memories that you could choose to lose or keep, so instead of arguing, instead of pushing the camera back toward her, you pulled it close when she let go of your hands and allowed her arms to fall back to the sides of her extravagantly embroidered white gown with its train of bleached peacock feathers. You wondered if they were real. They must have been. And you wondered how many peacocks had been killed to craft it.

"How was your trip here?" you asked after a moment, before the bride left, hoping that this might be a safe enough question for her to answer. Even if she couldn't respond when you'd asked that bold and direct question from before, perhaps this, she could. You wanted to hear her speak again, in Fuzhounese.

She seemed almost apologetic when she said, "It was . . . long and far."

"Oh, I see," was all you could muster before the bride flitted away again, almost too eagerly after seeing the disappointment on your face. But you held onto the sound of her voice and knew, since you were laid off, it was no longer something the factory could take from you, even if it wanted to.

At the back of the room, you spotted the only robotic member of the party, a rented android fortune teller sitting in a retro booth. With your camera, you wandered over as you'd seen many of the guests do throughout the night.

For each that had approached the android and asked for their fortune, you knew the machine had certainly scraped the web and their socials to gather information to craft likely fortunes, using pasts and presents to make it seem as though it could truly tell the future, but really, it probably only offered vague tidbits that had already occurred in the askers' lives and would likely occur again—privacy didn't exist and everyone knew that but pretended not to. You wondered how often the guests updated their socials, if they had been doing so all throughout the wedding. Your own profile hadn't been touched since you left. *Couldn't* be touched. Your photos were still from a time long past, holding images of a you long gone. And in the far reaches of your private grid, the family photo holding a ba who you could never again hope to find and a ma and mei who would be staring at the same photo framed at home, thinking the same of you.

If the android analyzed your profiles, it would only be able to see a person who existed in the past and no longer existed. You were convinced your fortune wouldn't be accurate. You didn't believe in such things anyhow, so you stepped past the fortune teller to what stood behind, what you were really after.

There was a tall, floor-to-ceiling door made of glass, swung outward to reveal the night. In the distance, you could see the scatter of lights from the mainland, toward home, far fewer than before, but maybe it was because it was nighttime, and it felt like a luxury that you got to see a glimpse of the home you left behind.

When packing for the floating city, your ma had remembered everything except the disposable camera you used to take photos of the mountains and your family. Your ma always reminded you to one day bring it into the city to process the film when you left, but you never had a chance to, and ultimately, all of you had forgotten when the time finally came.

You thought about snapping a photo of that clear but faint skyline but didn't.

Before you left, the bride transferred you the promised amount for your work, and it was generous, but not enough for you to afford a train ticket back home in time for New Year's. You'd have to wait another year, unless—

HOME

When you said you were leaving, your mei said she hated you for it, and your ma tried to explain to her why you had to go, but she wouldn't listen, wouldn't understand, or maybe it was you who didn't understand, what it was like to lose someone you loved and trusted so much only to have them betray you through an act that you yourself didn't think was significant. But in your mei's eyes—someone who had seen so little of the world, and you had made up so much of it—you could understand now, how catastrophic it must have been when she reluctantly sent you off at the train port with a grimace that held back the blubbering sobs you knew would rack her small body as soon as you turned with a one-way ticket clutched in your hand.

You knew exactly how your mei felt because your ba had done the same thing. Gained your trust, then broke it. But you know now that choice wasn't completely his alone.

You turned before you could see your ma or mei cry because you couldn't bear the tears, knew if you saw them then you'd cry too, and you didn't want that, because then you wouldn't leave, and you needed to leave, even if you didn't want to.

You remembered the times your mei and you fought, and how all those arguments seemed so insignificant now. Quibbling over things like who ate the last apple—

THE FLOATING CITY

There were adverts that floated along the sides of buildings, over streetlights along the almost empty roads. Holographic dancers in ancient Chinese fairy costumes and New Year lions twirled and leaped through the air—intangible heritage that had been slowly lost over time, and what was left was generated recordings, at least it seemed that way in the floating city. Below them hovered a feast with steam wafting upward. You could smell the roasted duck and pigs' feet even though you knew they weren't real.

Though there was no curfew, most didn't leave their rooms at night or stay out late because more often than not, they were too exhausted from work. But not you, not today. Well, you were exhausted, yes, but there were only three days until the trains would leave for the mainland, and you had no time left.

When you left your unit, of course, luck wasn't on your side. It didn't rain often in the floating city, but when it did, it was weighted and painful with droplets larger than grapes you hadn't seen nor eaten in years. It would help mask your presence, yes, but it didn't matter even if it wasn't raining because you'd made sure the security bots roaming the streets couldn't detect your worker identification barcode. There was a trick with oil, where you'd once accidentally rubbed it on your neck where the code sat, and upon returning to your unit after work, it hadn't detected that you'd entered, and you were almost reported as missing.

There were some inhabitants in the floating city who owned hover cars if their workplace was on the opposite side of where everyone resided. The parking lot was where you were headed.

When you arrived, you went for the hover car on the lowest stacked level, all those above towered like bookshelf displays, with the vehicles centered on each separate column. It was owned by the uncle three doors down from you, and you had seen him with a red envelope sticking out of his jacket pocket when he left for work this morning, and you only hoped he'd left it in his car in preparation for the trip back to the mainland.

The uncle's car was in sentry mode when you approached, though there were no cameras. Like the bots, they were made to detect identification codes only, thought to be safe enough to prevent thieves. And it had been, until now. Or at least you hoped you'd be the first to be successful.

There was a manual way of opening the car, a hidden keyhole in case identity unlocking wasn't functioning properly, and you had picked your fair share of locks because your ma often would forget the key to your family's home. This was a necessary crime—at least that was what you told yourself, rationalized it over and over in your mind so your courage, determination, and resolve wouldn't waver, as you crouched, picking at the lock before hearing a very firm click.

When you hopped into the car, you knew it was impossible to mask your presence by lingering behind, to clean up the slough of rain you brought in, dripping from your clothing. Your soaked running shoes squeaked against the mat beneath. The climate control of the car automatically began, blasting heat in your direction. You didn't have much time because the uncle would certainly be notified of the car turning on, if not the break-in. The stench of must and sour sweat filled the car, reminding you that you'd forgotten to shower the last two days.

Nearby, a security bot floated and halted, its eye narrowed in your direction as you held your breath, held still though your spine trembled from the cold. The bot closed in a few feet more as if staring directly at you before suddenly turning away.

Reanimated, you looked around the car for the red envelopes, adrenaline pulsing through you, warming your cheeks, but there was nothing in sight until you realized to open the dash. And there it was, a single red envelope decorated with a golden snake. Your hand quivered at the sight, and you thought about all the red envelopes your parents and relatives had given you over the years back home. It was never much, but to you, it was more than enough.

As you sat clutching the red pocket in your hand, your mind at war about whether to steal it or to leave it behind, you thought about how this could be for a child waiting eagerly for the uncle's return, an elder who could no longer earn their own pocket money, perhaps it might even be for his wife who he might have been working on the floating city to send money back to. You'd never know, and you tried not to think about it either because the guilty thoughts made your hands tremble, your resolve waver. Your head knocked back against the headrest of the driver's seat.

What a foolish plan this was. You almost laughed at yourself for your absurdity and desperation, but could you really be blamed for wanting to see your family? But could you really rob this of an uncle you didn't even know because of your selfish desire?

In the end, you decided to leave it behind, but not before opening it to peek at what was inside. You hadn't seen a red envelope like this for a long while.

Inside the envelope wasn't cash nor a check but a neatly folded letter. One written on paper, and it reminded you of the Polaroids and the camera and of the bride and of the Fuzhounese she spoke.

Then, you placed the envelope back into the dash, closed it, and stepped out of the car. But it didn't matter that you didn't follow through with the crime you set out to commit, because suddenly you were surrounded by the security bots, or maybe you were waiting to be caught all along.

At the security center, not even a real human was here to see you in the shadowed interrogation room with a single hanging light that reminded you a bit too much of the ones present at the wedding ceremony, and a plastic table that seemed as though they'd spent all the money on the light and didn't want to bother with something else expensive. Across from you was a bot, one too similar a size to you so that its eyeless metal face leveled with your own. You were sure this was on purpose. You were sure they customized the size of these bots in a way that would intimidate those sitting on the other side most.

"Why did you break into the car?"

You contemplated your answer but, drenched and dripping in the seat with your temperature cooling at a rapid rate, you couldn't care less to weave deception, so instead, you reached for the truth to see where it would take you. Regardless, you wouldn't be going home for New Year's. Within, you felt the same bold courage you had when you asked the bride about the world outside the floating island, when you asked her about your family.

"To steal." This time, your words were clear, enunciated, rather than a quiet murmur.

And as the words left you, instead of anxiety, you felt a certain sense of relief, but also the daunting pressure of defeat as your shoulders sagged further. Your eyes closed, you leaned back, and you imagined yourself back in the car with the heat blasting, and you were almost comforted by the memory.

"Why?" the bot asked, dragging you back to reality.

"I need money for the train. For New Year's."

"Do you not have enough?"

"I don't."

The bot paused, and several lines flickered across its face in a sort of pattern you couldn't read.

"But according to our records, you have at least a year's worth of income."

"I—what?"

In your mind, the bot showed you the records. It was correct. It was there. A partial portion of the money you'd sent back to your ma and mei. But it was not in your account, but the one of your family's. It seemed they had transferred to you the ownership, and of course, there was no way you'd be notified of such a thing. Not while you were in the floating city. You almost laughed because this was how you found out. But instead, a sob bubbled within you and left in a racking heave, and you couldn't help but wonder if your mei had cried the same way when you left.

Before you could catch your breath, the bot rose and left the room, waiting for you by the entrance that slid open. With weak steps, you followed behind the bot as it wandered down to the well-lit lobby that resembled more a hotel than any sort of police station.

You were let go with a warning because of your clean record so far, and your break-in was written off as an incident of misunderstanding, and you couldn't tell if you were simply being shown mercy, pity, or because they still needed you for something in the city even though you'd been laid off. You couldn't tell which was better and which was worse.

Or maybe it was the uncle who asked not to press charges—that might be the worst of all, because suddenly you felt as though you were twelve and caught stealing treats from your mei.

Your questions were answered as soon as you stepped out of the station and saw the uncle's car pulling out of the lot.

SNAKE #10

You got the ticket from Zodiac Travel Lines, and you're now nestled in one of the lowest-cost economy seats at the back of the SNAKE #10. You didn't want to use all the money that had come into your ownership because it had been meant for your ma and mei. They might've still needed it, and you'd convince them to spend it. To use it on your mei's education, to go toward that art studio your ma always joked about wanting, but both you and your mei knew it was no joke.

As you watched the floating city grow smaller in the distance, the tracks a long stretch across calm seas, you thought about how you hadn't seen your family in five years. The train was bringing you back to a past, a world you'd left behind, and you were afraid to witness how much it had changed without you, and how it would view you now that you'd, too, changed without it.

You kept your eyes closed until you arrived at your destination, which only seemed like seconds later, and you refused to look out the window as you collected your belongings, the Polaroid camera in hand, and stepped off the train while staring at your feet. With a long, deep breath and a shiver from the cold, only then did you look up. But now that you finally did, it seemed it hadn't only been five years since you left, because it looked as though the mainland had seen at least an entire generation gone past.

In the place of the glorious mountains and the villages that once rested below them were towering skyscrapers, so densely packed together that you could barely see between them or the clouds above them. Everything was in shades of blue: royal, cerulean, azure, aqua. Your hometown was devoid of the gentle trickle of streams, the dogs and chickens calling from the mountains, the dirt roads, and snugly nestled clay and brick homes.

That was when you realized why the mind mine needed such intricate details of the mountains from your mind, from the minds of all those who arrived at the floating city before you—so they could destroy that beautiful memory in reality and turn it into a memory of their own.

That was when you realized, time passed differently on the floating city. Slower, much slower, and you wished for the opposite—that it passed quicker, so that when you returned, what you would be returning to was a home that remained exactly the same, as though you'd never left it, with your ma and mei still standing at the train station, with your mei still crying, so that when she turned around, you'd be right there, and she'd run into your arms, asking you where you'd gone even though it would've only been minutes, or even seconds, and you'd tell her you'd never leave again and willed it to be true even if it wasn't, because dreams and realities almost never aligned, no matter how much you wanted them to.

You thought about how, when Ma said goodbye to you when you'd left, it sounded so final, as though she knew you wouldn't come back, just like Ba, or perhaps she knew all along that she wouldn't be there when you returned. Parents were like that, weren't they, always holding the most painful things from you until you stumbled upon those lessons on your own?

A notification pinged in front of your eyes as the train pulled away behind you.

Journey complete. Would you like to book your return passage?

There was enough money for a return ticket. You could go back to the floating city, continue to work, but then, who would you be living for there? Yet, who was there to live for here in the place you no longer recognized?

You clicked away on the notification and refocused on what was in front of you.

Then, you murmured the bride's words to yourself: *memories are only valuable if they can be lost.* With the camera raised, you pointed it toward what was left of the mountain you once remembered and snapped a photo of what had become of your home, now a stranger, praying that when the image developed, your ma, ba, and mei would be standing together within it, at the summit of mountains that had been felled and flattened—a memory upon so many other memories turned to rubble, not just your own.

Happy New Year, you whispered in Fuzhounese to the mountains. *I've returned.*

ABOUT THE AUTHOR

Ai Jiang is a Chinese-Canadian writer, Ignyte, Bram Stoker, and Nebula Award winner, and Hugo, Astounding, Locus, Aurora, and BSFA Award finalist from Changle, Fujian currently residing in Toronto, Ontario. Her work can be found in *F&SF, The Dark, The Masters Review,* among others. She is the recipient of Odyssey Workshop's 2022 Fresh Voices Scholarship and the author of *A Palace Near the Wind, Linghun,* and *I AM AI.*

Sea of Fertility

BELLA HAN

My big brother vanished in the virtual city of Laputa, leaving no trace behind. I sit up, sweating, for a moment convinced I'm still dreaming. Feed globes drift in, flooding my vision with news. The man beside me opens his eyes, about to speak, but teleports away at my gloomy expression. I've forgotten his username.

I wave off the auto-generated music and get out of bed, stepping onto a mess of candy wrappers. The only thing I remember from last night is the Senso candies—the latest masterwork I created in the lab, featuring an exceptional sensation of pain. But they're still missing something. I know that—I always know that they're no match for real feelings. I had wanted to ask Brother for suggestions, even though he never liked my research. But just now, before I was fully awake, the system asked me, "Who is your brother?"

I reach out to search manually. My smart choker glows, and a search icon appears in the air. "Weilan Yu," I say his name.

Data streams through the transparent choker while the translucent icon spins dizzily. After a moment, words appear:

"User not found."

My heart sinks. I search for his current username, "Azure," then his former one, "Ray." No results. Nothing on his band, "Polar Day," or his music. No past interactions with him in my social history. No trace of his user ID. Brother has evaporated from the city of Laputa, as if he never existed.

My hand drops. Through the panoramic windows, cloud shadows shifted across my face. Beyond this empty room lies a city of eternal daytime. From this height, the view is dominated by a colossal ember-shaped building, followed by a tower that rises like clustered crystal. At the bases of the skyscrapers, Eighth Avenue swarms with people, flowing like a river of pixels. Hot topics rise like balloons, filling the sky, while outdated ones fall like shooting stars. The sky is perpetually blue, crowned with radiant summer clouds. This is Laputa, the greatest city ever built.

But now, a bug has been revealed. People don't vanish in Laputa. If they go bankrupt, their names are struck through, and they start over with a new account. If they die, their names turn gray. A twinge of anxiety pricks me—it's been a while since I last felt anything this strong. No, it can't be serious. Brother must be playing a new trick.

I dash to the wall, which transforms into a mirror, displaying all my available looks. I tap my favorite and shift into it: a high ponytail, a sporty-chic dress, and sneakers.

"To Brother's," I command.

"ERROR: LINK BROKEN."

The warning appears in the air, then fades like traces of rain.

Of course. I let out a dry laugh. I don't remember the coordinates of his apartment, but at least—I glance at the urban labyrinth and command, "To Stellar Plaza"—I know how to get there *on foot.*

When I arrived at Laputa for college, Brother showed me around the city. Back then, he was called Ray, and there was a light in his eyes. He wore a cool bomber jacket, while I was stuck with the goofy default jumpsuit. Starting from Stellar Plaza, we set off to see the world.

Buildings rose into the sky, gleaming like gems. Twelve spotlight avenues radiated from the Plaza, bustling with all kinds of weirdos, some not even human. People paraded along the roads, each step paired with a sweet tinkling in the air. Fun topics danced in the clouds, while Off-islands dotted the sky like a planetary ring. I couldn't help bouncing with excitement, and Brother couldn't hide his smile. "See? This is the paradise we dreamed of as kids!"

Seven years passed since then, and the city has changed. Along Second Avenue, skyscrapers crystallize overnight, only to dissolve months later. The Horn of Plenty is gone, replaced by the fancier, pricier Carat. Story Factory has vanished, along with its successor, Black Light Theater, replaced by Shard Gallery, a twisted mirror of a building.

The only familiar sight is Sand Tower. I was among the first students to attend this college, but now, it's a rite of passage for every teenager to earn their first batch of Value Points here. So the spiral tower keeps growing, looming so tall it might fall at any moment.

The Tower's research institutes are scattered across the city, shaped like seashells. My workplace on Third Avenue resembles a nautilus. The

Sensory Center: the cornerstone of today's Laputa. It pioneered and perfected the simulation of sensations that furnish the city. Our lab has taken it a step further, producing feelings directly through programming. It's an art that demands imagination more than technique, and its byproducts, the Senso candies, ensure steady cash flow for the lab. I've designed some bestsellers myself, but now, I'm becoming increasingly unsure what feelings truly are.

I trot through the crowd. Silent loners trudge by, poker-faced, glancing at feed globes, voting Love or Hate on hot topics, raising or lowering someone's Value Points. I used to be one of them, but now the topics feel meaningless and the whole concept somehow off. When I bump into someone, their virtual body flickers and glitches, the spot I almost touched dissolving into mist. I haven't requested to *link* with any of them, so naturally, we can't interact physically.

I stride through the crowd like wading through ghosts. A teddy bear gets jostled. Its virtual form disrupted, and it swears so crudely the auto-interpreter refuses to translate. Now it threatens to beat me up. Let it try—it can't touch me anyway. In an instant, glowing golden triangles appear on its body, freezing it in place. See? Logos has stepped in.

I glance at Logos Tower. The tallest building in Laputa, it's a black obelisk crowned with a golden pyramid. Logos Inc. built and runs the city, overseeing everything and tending to everyone. Beneath the blue sky, the black obelisk absorbs light while the golden pyramid dazzles my eyes.

I turn onto a side street. Beneath the railings, water glimmers in psychedelic hues, submerging the bases of skyscrapers. But it's not water—it's digital trash. The city's data, once left to decay, weathers into quicksand. As the sea of quicksand rises, the city sinks, and the skyscrapers must grow taller. It's said there's a world under water, but I have no interest in that adventure.

Here it is. Sandwiched between high-rises, Brother's apartment looks like a small piece of sea glass. He once lived in a Vassal Apartment just like I do, enduring advertisements and regulations instead of paying. But soon he said he couldn't be a "vassal" anymore and emptied his pockets for a small apartment of his own. These independent apartments are now relics; no one bothers to waste time and Value Points arranging every pixel of their room when everything is ready and free in a Vassal Apartment.

I walk into the hall and step into a beam of light. AZ255—glad I still remember the room number. The light transforms into a panoramic elevator, and the city shrinks beneath my feet. This special effect mirrors the developer's slogan, "A REAL HOME in the cyber world."

Brother's place felt like home more than anyone else's. Apartments usually consist of only a bedroom, but he created a family room just for me. Rain streamed along glass walls, creating soothing sounds. Bookshelves were filled with encyclopedias, mineral samples, toys, musical instruments—souvenirs from our childhood. Two beanbags lay on the wooden floor, scattered with books and scraps of paper.

Books had become endangered, for no one, except Brother, could stare at plain text for more than five minutes. Papers were scribbled with obscure sentences—probably Brother's poems. I once asked why he still wrote poems in an era like this, and he replied, "Words are dead, so poetry once again becomes mysterious. Poets become priests and priestesses again, praying for whatever power they might possess . . . "

There was a soothing scent in the room. Warm, moist, and a little dusty, a wonderful mix of simulated smells. I miss that scent. When I see Brother, I'll ask what trick he is playing, or maybe file a complaint to Logos on his behalf, then wish him a happy birthday. It's been so long since we last met.

Ding! The elevator has arrived. I see a door in the cement wall, not blue as I remember. It opens without verifying my identity.

There is no familiar scent.

There is nothing but bare concrete. As I step in, the room shifts into a demo, cycling through interior designs including minimalist, luxurious, avant-garde, and classical. Cheerful music playing, I step on colorful tiles, walk past ever-changing sofas, paintings, and decorations, and reach the end of the room. The demo fades, revealing the concrete frame. Winds mess my hair as a shining city stretches out beneath my feet. Feed globes swarm up, advertising "a REAL HOME in the cyber world." I crouch down, burying my face in my knees.

The man crushes Senso candies between his teeth, fumes rising from his mouth. He digs another handful from the jar and swallows them whole. The color tells me he is eating our bestseller, Igniite®. Overdosing won't harm his body—it's virtual and can be rebooted anytime. But I'm not sure what it'll do to his mind. I barely recognize him, yet I know this demeanor.

"Azure's little sis, aren't you?" Vol snaps his eyes open, sweating.

Brother calls him Volcano. "Among all bassists in Laputa, Volcano is *the* best," he once said. They released an album two years ago. But today, Vol is no longer the man I knew. He's changed his brown eyes to chrome green, his dirty blond hair an exquisite slate green. He stands coldly beautiful in designer suits, the laser logo of his new band flashing on his back. All these alterations must have been couture, costing a fortune.

Backstage, programming interfaces float in the air, while on the front stage, antique instruments like guitars and drums are on display. Mechanical components hang above our heads, forming two monstrous creatures—Fujin and Raijin, gods of wind and lightning, as Lapupedia tells me. This is Club Phanta, where Brother played many times when it wasn't this fancy. Now, its white stage rises like a cliff, separating the band from an audience of millions. Drumbeats pulse through the heated air—an air our Sensory Center proudly presents.

Vol snatches back the Link Request (*Vol wants to link with you tonight!*) he just sent me. Anyone else might see it as a humiliation—but not me. Not today.

"You guys quarreled again?" I ask.

"Ah. That man doesn't quarrel with me." Vol picks up his bass and fiddles with it. "It was just a difference of ideas."

Ah, that again. Well, at least they'd lasted two years; most bands don't make it that far. Then again, Brother was always the first to piss off his bandmates.

"So, what did he say?"

Vol's voice is muffled by a jumble of notes. " . . . Lifeless."

"What?"

"He said my music was LIFELESS!" Vol glares at me. "Told me to show him some proof of life. Bullshit! He's got talent, he's got a pretty face, so he can say that. But what do I have? Well, I've got a good punch for him if he's still around."

Crack. He smashes a candy between his teeth.

"A year. A whole year, and we didn't come up with a single track. He was never satisfied with anything we struggled to make. He used to make games and earn Points, so he didn't care. But I had to. Did he know I was taking on beginner's tasks just to survive, like some kid fresh out of Sand Tower? Did he know how few Love Votes we got? . . . Let's face it. No one needs music anymore. Not everyone can live like him, putting his heart into his music—not to mention he himself can't come up with anything. Us common folks, we have our own ways of life . . . "

He presses his forehead against the bass, the laughter of his new mates ringing out behind him.

"So you broke up with him?" I ask.

"Yeah, I did," he murmurs, his green eyes calm as chrome. "Before he could ditch me first."

Of course. What else could he do? In times like these, who needs to cling to anyone? Thanks to the invention of the Link Request, I haven't made that foolish attempt in years. But why, why am I trying so hard to find my brother today?

"Do you know where he went?"

"Who knows. Probably dragging someone into his next stupid album. I've told him a thousand times, no one listens to albums anymore. Told him he'd go bankrupt if he kept making them. He never listened."

Looking at him, I hesitate to tell him that Brother disappeared. The show is about to begin; the band steps up to their instruments without even touching them.

"Don't you tune your instruments first?" I ask, confused.

"Oh, we don't," Vol sneers. "Those are all dummies. Who cares about playing grandpa instruments?"

"But—but isn't that your selling point?"

"You think they can tell the difference?" He tilts his chin at the audience. "Well, doesn't matter if they can. They don't come for that anyway. They come for this air—the company paid a fortune for it. Smell it!" He lifts his head. "The scent of beer, sweat, and grass. The heat that makes your pulse race, like those summer nights when you were sixteen. Look at these people—they love me. These are the proofs of my life."

He opens his arms. The lights go out, Fujin and Raijin glow, the darkness blazes, the crowd goes frenetic, and Love Votes multiply at the speed of sound.

Some people know Brother better than he knows himself. They know that, uninterested in perfecting his virtual body, he has a tiny acne scar on his face. They know which designer, from which season, created Brother's iconic misty blue coat. Take this girl, for example. She is so famous that I can find her with a quick search: hot pink hair, trendy outfits, following one superstar after another, spending countless Value Points to support them, and earning even more from her own fans. Desiree, "the star-chasing Queen," is the founder of Brother's fan club. Strange, considering Brother barely counts as a star.

At the top of the Carat, panoramic windows wrap around the rotunda, tinting the sky with an imaginary dusk. Watercolor tiles form a Venus de Milo, while languid music and diamond sparkles float through the air. I'm out of place here, as every other table holds a companion—the same companion. A young blond man, handsome like sunshine, melts his date with just a grin. Lapupedia tells me he's Vitamin, the latest virtual idol.

With their dates, a dozen Vitamins exchange loving glances, share drinks with heart-shaped straws, or wipe cake crumbs from their dates' lips. I wrinkle my nose and look away just as Desiree arrives, stepping right on the face of the mosaicked Venus.

She looks like a teenager. Her shiny pink hair is tied into two pointy buns; her iridescent dress catches the light like a candy wrapper. Slumping and flicking her hair back, she exclaims, "My limited-edition date is ruined! I wouldn't forgive you if you weren't Azure's sister. So tell me, why didn't you reach out until now?"

"Until now?" I echo.

She stares at me from behind bushes of eyeshadow. "Your brother disappeared two weeks ago. Didn't you know?"

I'm speechless. No, I didn't, because I haven't been in touch with him for a long time. What was I busy with? I can't remember. Research, killing time, linking with someone tonight just to say goodbye tomorrow, drowning happily in my pointless life.

"I was busy with . . . something."

She sighs. "Those days were a nightmare. He vanished into thin air, along with all the archives we kept. The club went mad; I cried every day, complained to Logos, asked for help everywhere, but got no replies. I had all the club members searching for him, but he's always been so discreet . . . "

"Do you know where he's been lately?"

She shakes her head. "Since parting with Vol, he hasn't shown up or said anything in public—until six months ago. He said he was working on a new album at a 'secret base,' but no one knows where that is."

"Let me help with the search." I offer, "I know a bit about him—or at least I think so . . . "

"Thanks, but no." She smiles bitterly. "We've given up."

"—Given up?" I grasp the table so tightly my knuckles turn white. "But it's only been two weeks! Don't you guys claim to lov—"

"Yeah. I haven't been this crazy about anyone since I was younger." She leans back in the chair, desolation flickering across her eyes. How old is she, really?

"He wasn't my type," she continues. "Wasn't famous, hadn't perfected his looks, and was a little weird, to be honest. But when I heard his music on a show, it was like being sucked into a black hole, and I saw something I'd lost long ago . . .

"At first, it was just another game for me; he was handsome enough anyway. But soon I couldn't stop listening to his music or sending him Link Requests. When he finally accepted, it hit me all at once that it was over. I couldn't get any closer to him. Funny, isn't it? In a time like this, longing for that archaic 'connection' again . . .

"So when fate told me, 'Go back to your old joys,' I disbanded the fan club. No one objected."

I have nothing to say. Desiree snaps her fingers, and Vitamin the Virtual Idol appears like magic. Glancing back, I see him tenderly wiping cake crumbs from her lips.

There was a special member in the fan club who recommended Brother's music in his show. Tetsu, a celebrity host, runs *The Best of Life*, a show that covers everything from the best wine to the best philosophy. I've watched the show a few times: a charming man in his thirties speaks with passion, ease, and a sexy accent, making it incredibly addictive. Now I sit on his sofa, waiting for my coffee.

The cosmic gray sofa feels as smooth as cream. The crystal tea table bends light like a prism. Beyond the panorama windows lies the city of Laputa—I've never seen it from this height, and it almost scares me. Sunlight pours over the wall, where photo frames display the subject of each episode: the best game, the best restaurant, the best high heels, and the best . . . Senso candy. Clearly, the owner of this apartment has a taste for our classic, Cloud9®.

He's busy in the kitchen, where cooking machines and utensils shine coldly—things you wouldn't find in ordinary apartments. Rumbling, rattling, boiling, trickling, and a sweet aroma fill the air. I want to say, *Please, save me the trouble; it's all patched together with gustatory simulations anyway,* but I hold my tongue. Tetsu returns with two cups of coffee.

He looks exactly like he does on the show: bronze skin, stylish hair and stubble, chic glasses, and an exquisite gray suit. He sits down, and wiggles his finger, and elegant music starts to play.

I pick up the cup and spot a monster on the saucer. A woman's head, a lion's body, and a bird's wings. *Sphinx*—Lapupedia identifies it instantly. The coffee is slightly bitter, slightly sour, and slightly sweet. I can't describe it beyond that, as I'm no expert on simulated gustation.

"Nice," Tetsu remarks. "A flawless echo of the original beans, resurrecting their radiant aroma and exquisitely orchestrated flavors. No wonder it remains the most celebrated work of simulated coffee. What do you think? And how about the music?"

"It's fine."

His light gray eyes fix on me, making my hair stand on end.

"It's fine?" The man raises an eyebrow. "No, you don't like it. I don't like it either. I've subscribed to the most expensive music service, which promises all human-made pieces, but I haven't heard much humanity in them." He puts down his cup with a thud. "The best music has vanished. I featured it on my show once, only to earn more Hate Votes than Love Votes because the audience hates any changes. The director AI warned me not to be 'capricious' again. To hell with it."

Collapsing onto the sofa, he mutters, "I hate my show."

His personality is not quite what I imagined.

"Tetsu," I ask as he gathers and shuffles through the Link Requests he's received today. "Do you know where the 'secret base' is?"

"I can only guess." He picks up a Request, examines it, then tosses it aside. "Under water, maybe. I've heard stories about the people there—that they can erase traces. If Azure pissed off someone like that . . . "

I don't dare imagine what could happen.

"But there's another possibility," he continues. "If Azure managed to build a secret base under water, he could erase his traces on his own. He's disappointed in the city—I can tell from his lyrics. I'm disappointed too, yet all I do is complain. But Azure is a poet. A poet would erase everything to break up with the world. A poet might even erase himself—"

"No he wouldn't," I interrupt. "He wouldn't abandon me, his sister."

So I say, selfishly. When the truth is, I'm the one who abandoned him.

Tetsu stares at me as if I've said something incomprehensible. "Miss Lazuli . . . "

"Yes?"

"What do blood ties mean? I know the definition, but I still don't understand. Is someone important to me just because we share blood?"

This man, this sophisticated, charismatic man on stage, now looks like a lost child. Suddenly, it dawns on me. Tetsu doesn't understand blood ties because he was born after the invention of artificial wombs, just sixteen years ago. He is a genius actor, but a lonely human. I've become one too, starting today.

Tetsu throws all the Link Requests into the air and sinks into the sofa. The photo frames cast heavy shadows over him, as if trying to crush him.

"How should I live my life from tomorrow?" he mutters.

At the end of Twelfth Avenue stands a digital paradise. The closer you get, the smaller and scarcer the buildings become. It's late, yet the sky never darkens in this city. Sunlight dances on the quicksand sea, its color kaleidoscopic. In a district nicknamed "Thirteenth Avenue," a massive soap bubble floats on the sea with glowing words: *Les Enfants du Paradis.*

I merge into the bubble. In the deep ocean blue, millions of jellyfish drift, each carrying a fluorescent name. When a citizen dies in reality, a new jellyfish appears in this paradise. The living can rent a bubble beside the jellyfish to display the digital traces of the deceased. Bubbles rise, jellyfish dance; I reach out, only to grab emptiness.

Brother's name isn't here; he isn't dead. But what if, in Laputa's eyes, he's never lived? His name won't appear here, and his existence will dissolve like a bubble that failed to pay its lease. Will there come a day when I keep a jellyfish for him in my apartment and simply move on?

I can't remember a single poem he wrote.

The alarm clock rings. It's time for all of us to return to the flesh, to that dull eight-hour dream of eating, exercising, cleaning, and sleeping, all alone as always.

When he was "Ray," Brother was among Laputa's first game artisans, and I was his first player. He started making a game on a whim, never expecting to work on it day and night—or for it to blow up. *Ciel* is the adventure of a boy flying through a strangely beautiful world. No other place fulfills humanity's dream of flight better than Laputa; in this game, you experience the full thrill of flying with your own virtual body. I knew the game would be a hit before it was finished; sure enough, many of my classmates got so hooked they barely passed that year.

But the following year, after producing a sequel with bigger funding and better tech, Brother declared he was done and never touched the game engine again.

"Didn't you say games are Laputa's greatest magic?" I asked.

"Yes, but it's already fading," he replied.

Six months ago, I received a key. Antique in shape, black as if swallowing light, with *Voise* engraved on it. It might be the key to a game called *Voise*, but I found no trace of it or the sender. Today, I have a theory.

I call on my apartment wall to display my digital assets. After some rummaging, I find what I'm looking for. I pick the key's image, and it turns 3D in my hand, cold and heavy. If I'm right, it could be my lighthouse to Brother.

Since graduation, we've spoken less and less. The last time I reached out was to wish him a happy birthday. With fewer and fewer replies from me, Brother eventually lost heart. This key might be his last attempt.

Countless Off-islands gleam in the sky, each a game universe. This is Infinite Wonderland, the biggest provider of happiness for the city. But in my eyes, this vibrant cosmos is dulling, just as Brother had prophesied.

I fly through the Gate of Bliss into the Temple of Joy, standing in a resplendent hall with the black key in hand.

Beneath the dome, an apsara sits in the lotus position, her hands forming gestures, two others holding treasures; her hair and garments flutter, her smile serene. Billions of discs spin inside the dome, each a live thumbnail and a portal to a game. Each hums its own noise, harmonized by the system into celestial music. I step forward, and the discs rearrange themselves to match my preferences.

The apsara raises her loving eyes, "Are you worried, dear? All worries are like dreams and illusions, like dews and lightning—better forgotten." She opens her hand, and a lotus blooms within, revealing the latest games.

"I'm worried, and I want to file a complaint." I reply.

"About?"

I raise the key. "I bought this game but haven't played it yet. Today, I wanted to give it a try, but I couldn't find its entrance. You have to help me."

Data flickers through her eyes as she takes the key. "I'm sorry," the apsara says. "There's no such game in our database."

"Nonsense!" I stamp my foot, "Are you telling me the game ran away on its own? Do I have to play hide-and-seek before playing your games?"

She smiles and explains, "As a player of trendy games, you may not have encountered this before, Miss Lazuli. Infinite Wonderland isn't truly infinite. When a game underperforms, it's removed from our Off-islands—deleted from our database, in other words. In this case, we recommend seeking help in the Hall of Harmony; some players might have backups in their personal space. Otherwise, we can issue you a refund at any time. Sometimes, it's best to move on. These new games have been specially selected for you: *Shadow Warrior, Suspiria, Eyes Wide Shut* . . . "

"Enough," I interrupt. "Just send me to the Hall of Harmony."

She waves her finger, and I plunge into a copper-red ocean.

The Hall of Harmony lies beneath the Temple of Joy, a place designed for discussion. I descend past topics, feed globes, and players—chatting, quarreling, and striking deals—into the shadowy depths of this hemispherical space. My feet sink into quicksand, the remains of topics gone cold.

During this trip, I've found nothing useful. So I call out, "Anyone know a game called *Voise*?"

The topic rises like a bubble. People teleport in, take quick glances, and teleport away. It begins to sink.

"Any news about Ray, the creator of *Ciel*?" I shout again.

I wait in vain. The noise from above, harmonized by the system, melds into a strange symphony. Gripping the key, I trace its engravings with my finger. No one replies; they've forgotten him so quickly.

Someone tries to tap my shoulder, only to disrupt my virtual form. A figure in a hooded, transparent raincoat appears behind me. Beneath the coat, their body blurs like a phantom, revealing only a hand and part of their face. Three layers of geographic tattoos drift across their dark skin, rippling in electric violet, like a mirage. I'm mesmerized until a raincoat hits me in the face.

"Put it on," a woman's voice commands.

My body blurs beneath the coat as I slip into it. She tosses me a glowing anchor icon; I catch it, and a dazzling teleportation begins.

The landscapes shift endlessly, blending into a swirl of colors. In a blink, I fly across countless places. When I land, I find myself standing on an anchor symbol within a glowing circle. A dim corridor stretches ahead, illuminated by colorful droplets falling like rain. No, not raindrops—quicksand. The sand splashes onto my skin, burning me with the condensed information it carries.

"Sorry, the ceiling's leaking again," the woman says. She unbuttons her raincoat and pulls back her hood, revealing a pixie cut and catlike eyes. She's dressed in a tank top and denim shorts, her dark skin adorned with a mirage of tattoos. She hasn't erased the faint wrinkles from her face, which only add to her charm. On another day, I might have sent her a Request, but for now, I keep my distance—I can neither see her username nor access her profile.

She leads the way while I discreetly try to pinpoint our location. The coordinate marker has gone haywire; I call up the map, but it takes forever to load, only to display a blurry mosaic.

"Don't bother," the woman interrupts. "Most services don't work here. I'm Tondra."

The name means lightning. At least the auto-translation still functions.

"Where are we, Tondra? Why did you bring me here?"

She smiles, pouting her lips toward the ceiling. "Because we can't talk about certain things *up there*."

I glance at the dripping "raindrops," and it clicks. We're *under water*.

"And the raincoat? Just to keep the 'rain' off?" I ask.

"Oh, that's a new feature. The main purpose is to keep you hidden. Not even Logos can track you when you're wearing it. So remember, lil' sis—keep it on as long as you're under water."

She pushes open the heavy gates. Inside is a bar shrouded in darkness, a circular bar table glinting at the center, and feed globes glowing all around. Guests of all kinds, all in raincoats, strike secret deals with something silver. There's no background music, only whispers. Beyond the panoramic windows, a misty ocean of quicksand unfolds, the bases of skyscrapers looming in the distance.

We weave through the crowd to a sofa by the window. Tondra lounges like a queen as a bartender arrives with two cocktails: one a rosy purple, the other a deep blue. She plucks a candy ball from her drink and crushes it between her teeth. I decide it's better not to try mine.

"How do you know I'm Ray's sister?" I ask.

"Ray? Ray, the creator of *Ciel*?" She tilts her head. "No—aren't you Haze's sister? You look just like him, and you've got his key."

"Haze? Which Haze?"

"I'm not sure exactly what his name was. He said he was Haze, or Heize, or something like that, so that's what I called him. Even learning that name wasn't easy; he was so quiet."

"How did you get to know this Haze?"

She grins, violet smoke slipping from between her teeth. "Do you know what pirates are, little friend?"

I know pirates from games—smoky-eyed men and women, sailing and plundering. I don't think that's what she means.

"Pirates are robbers," she says, downing her cocktail, an anchor pendant flickering on her chest. "And it's Infinite Wonderland that I rob."

The pendant glows, and we're teleported to a new place, sofa and all. Beyond a glass dome, colorful waves crash overhead, the peaks of skyscrapers glitter far above. Inside the dome, billions of discs spin, each a portal to a game. A Nataraja stands beneath the dome—the divine dancer of the cosmos. Looking closer, I recognize many of the games, and the "Nataraja" turns out to be a male stripper. This is a parody wonderland, sailing beneath the waves.

"Welcome to the Black Pearl," the captain says, arms wide open.

"See, my money isn't clean. Here in the Black Pearl, users can access any game from Infinite Wonderland for free. But that's not enough—I have to offer games Wonderland doesn't have and wouldn't dare to provide. We've built a reputation, so about a year ago, that man brought me his work."

"I knew he was dangerous the moment he walked in. A cloud of information loomed over him, overloading your brain as you got close—like sinking your hand into quicksand. That was the smell of Senso cigs."

"Senso cigarettes?!"

I'd heard about them when I started working at the Sensory Center. A researcher was fired for leaking a dangerous lab experiment, and that was their prototype. They've driven countless people mad, sending them spiraling into White Eden. Compared to them, Senso candies are as tame as kittens. I can't believe Brother had anything to do with them.

"Senso cigarettes indeed," the pirate says, eyes lighting up. "I tried one once—it was called 'Breath of God,' as I recall. A rush of information that spun your head, paralyzed your body, and plunged you into a whirlpool of sounds, colors, sensations, emotions . . . all horribly alive. You'd see the city of Laputa, a symphony of data, and the smoke you exhaled, forming the face of God—and you'd melt into it, becoming God itself. When I woke up, I wanted to die, but you can't take lives in this city. I never touched the cigs again."

"But Haze . . . "

"Yes, he was a Senso junkie. What kind of game could someone like that bring me? But my sailors got hooked on his work, and I couldn't help but try it. It was called *Ekko.* Looked plain, didn't even tell a story, but I couldn't stop playing. Felt like I was losing my mind, like being watched by a beast in the dark . . . only to realize that poor creature was none other than myself."

She exhales a puff. "The game was a hit. After that, he kept bringing me games. I gave him his share, but we never talked. One day, I forced him to show his face and tell me his name. I saw a handsome young man—skinny, buzz cut, dressed stylishly in black, with deep shadows under his eyes. His features looked like yours."

But it wasn't my brother with soft, short fringes and the misty blue coat anymore.

The pirate continues, "I asked him why he made all these games; clearly not for Value Points. And he said, 'I don't know . . . I'm searching for an answer, but I don't know the question yet . . . ' and covered his eyes with his hands.

"After that, his games changed. One day, I found him lounging in my bar with a man and a woman in his arms, blowing smoke into their mouths. I threw his games at his face and told him to sell them to Wonderland; he could make good money. He bit the girl's lip, drawing blood, and she just giggled. He said, 'I gave up. Let them have what they want. What's wrong with seeking pleasure?'

"He didn't show up again until six months ago. He brought a game called *Voise* and said, 'This is the last game by Haze.'

"'Have you found the question?' I asked.

"'No,' he replied, 'but I met a ghost.'

"He told me to take care and disappeared into the dark. That was the last time I saw him—and the first time I saw him smile."

Game discs spin overhead as Tondra finishes her drink. In the smoke she exhales, Brother's face begins to blur in my mind. Turns out I didn't know him at all; I didn't even notice when he stopped smiling. The pirate studies my expression, tattoos glistening over her skin.

"End of the story," she announces. "Now, where's the storyteller's reward?"

I snap back to reality. She didn't come to me for charity; she'd been eyeing the black key from the start.

"You can't access that *Voise* game, can you?" I ask.

She shakes her head. "We don't have Off-islands, so our games are stored in the artisans' personal spaces, and they crash at times. Two weeks ago, all of Haze's games went down. Normally, we wouldn't care—but this was Haze. I had backups for all his games, but the backup for *Voise* was corrupted. We've nearly fixed it, except the keys he made. They seem to have some special features . . . "

I bite my lower lip. "What's in it for you? Making good money?"

"What's wrong with good money?" She smiles. "I've been waiting for him to take his share. But it seems he never will . . . "

"My brother disappeared," I cut in. "I give you the key, you give me the game. I'll bring him back."

Voise flies to me, transforming from a game disc into a keyhole. I insert the black key and turn it. The keyhole morphs into a doorway, and I step through.

I wake in darkness. It's tangible, spherical, and icy cold. Sounds have form, too, bouncing heavily in the void. I try to speak but find myself mute; yet I can wield sound as my weapon. I take a sharp sound, slashing open the darkness. It shatters into billions, scattering into deep space.

In a greater darkness, stars emerge. I take a loud sound as my canoe, a quiet one as my oar, and sail toward the distant stars. Fog blindfolds me, so I listen to the stars to navigate. Sound waves buffet my boat, forcing me to fight against the current.

A small planet shimmers ahead. A snow globe brimming with flowing, flowering sounds. Inside, a human figure floats, sleeping like a baby. I knock on the globe. No response. I try to slash it open, only to be engulfed by roaring flames. TRY AGAIN: like a hunter eyeing its prey; search for weaknesses, avoid the traps, choose the weapon, and strike. The globe shatters into a blizzard, releasing a heavenly chorus. Amid the shards, the little figure lies bleeding but still asleep.

I pick up the most beautiful fragment and carry it to my canoe. It's still singing. Suddenly, I can't lift my left foot—it has turned to stone.

Hunting is addictive. Each fragment I collect adds to my arsenal. Every time I destroy a planet, I grow more petrified—yet tougher. I haul all the fragments back to my birthplace to build a sanctuary, grander and more glorious than any other. Though incomplete, it already gleams with kaleidoscopic sounds. Dragging my heavily petrified body, I defeat the boss and bring back the final piece of sound.

The voices of all beings chant their cacophony. I place the last piece, completing my sanctuary. A pyramid at the center of the universe, incomparable and indestructible. All sounds and colors converge into an epic symphony; I rise and rotate at the heart of the sanctuary as it reaches its grand finale.

A decrescendo, a diminuendo. The last light fades, and I close my eyes. In the pyramid at the center of the universe, I'm completely turned to stone.

This is true darkness. I can't see, hear, speak, or move. I'm trapped inside myself, like a stray planet in space. Tondra told me this is the Normal End of the game. She didn't know if a True End existed—when the Black Pearl was last attacked, all the game's walkthroughs vanished. So I must either quit now or keep rotating for six, eight, or forty-eight hours, waiting for someone to break into this mausoleum and transform me into a beautiful new fragment.

No light. No sound. And I sleep.

No light. No . . .

A sound wakes me, but I still can't move this body of stone. It's as light as a feather, yet listen closely, and you'll feel its weight. It sounds like approaching footsteps. Like the fall of piano keys—I remember watching Brother play the piano as a child, his warm, peaceful notes filling the room. Like heartbeats. Like someone tenderly knocking at the door.

I push, squeeze, bump, and break free from this prison of stone. I drag my petrified muscles, part my cracking lips, and force a noise from my hoarse throat.

Darkness splits open. Someone approaches. A soft paw brushes against my eyes—then I can see. A polar bear, reaching out its hand to mine. I grasp that big, warm hand, and it leads me through the dark, across the stars, and into a snowy void.

I remember another warm hand. The year my parents divorced, I ran away to another city to find Brother but got lost in the snowy town. He found me, showed me around, and bought me candied hawthorn berries. When the adults found us, he couldn't let go of my hand. I looked at him, then at Mother and her new husband, and I understood. My sixteen-year-old brother was just a kid; he, too, wished for someone to hold his hand, guiding him through the snow.

At the end of the void, a blue door appears. The bear stops and turns to me. Suddenly, I understand, pulling the black key from my pocket. Together, we open the door.

Colors swirl, scenes shift, and I land in a bright room. The ceiling flickers and glitches, with colorful raindrops dripping onto white sand. Grotesque plants burst from the sand, while sea waves ebb and flow on the walls. I clutch the black key, unsure if I'm still in the game. A warning pops up, solving the mystery:

"ERROR: LINK FAILED. USER NOT FOUND."

My head spins. Where am I? Why this message? And when did I even request to link with anyone? I put the key back and try to access Lapupedia, only to remember the service doesn't work here.

I walk through the plants, listening to the sound of waves, unimpressed by the garden owner's taste. Don't they realize many people in Laputa suffer from phytophobia? Well, it's under water, and you meet all kinds of weirdos. Now I'm starting to feel a little anxious.

A bench sits in the center of the garden. I sit down, feeling trapped amid monstrous plants. Cacti, I recall—they're cacti. Someone is lurking behind the cacti.

"Who's there?!" I jump to my feet, frustrated at being bare-handed.

Gold and orange flicker between the greens. A young man steps out, hands raised. He's about my age, tall, slender, and blond, wearing an orange T-shirt beneath his raincoat. He takes a step forward, then flinches back; his cowardice irritates me.

"Are you . . . Are you Azure's sister?" he asks. "Do you know where he is?"

I pull back my hood. "Who are you? Why are you looking for my brother?"

He steps forward. With hazel eyes and freckles, he's quite cute, but not my type.

"I'm Jonny. I made music with Azure."

Well, Vol was right about what Brother was up to. We just didn't expect him to cooperate with a rookie. "What's this place?" I ask.

The young man smiles slightly, relaxing. "The secret base. Azure's."

God. I turn to a blazing cactus, poking at its plump leaves and feeling the sting. So vivid—but why had Brother blown so many Value Points on things like these? "I didn't know he'd developed such a taste," I murmur.

Jonny gazes at the cacti with affection. "I wondered why, too. But he said they reminded him of himself . . . "

I wrinkle my nose, doubting how these ugly plants could resemble my handsome brother. "How long have you known him?" I ask.

He bites his lower lip. "Not long—or very long, I'd say. Have you seen him lately, Azure's sister?"

"I have a name. Lazuli."

"Sorry," he mumbles, stepping closer, eyes eager. "Miss Lazuli, have you seen Weilan Yu lately?"

Gazing at him, I slowly shake my head. He staggers back like a dying flame, collapsing against a cactus.

"He's been gone for two weeks. I've been searching everywhere, from above water to under water . . . but I'm too useless to find a clue. Someone even scammed me out of all my Points, so now I have to do beginner's tasks every day just to keep this secret base . . . " He buries his face in his hands. "When I saw you, I thought there was hope, but . . . "

I pat the bench, inviting him to sit down. "I'm looking for him too. I got here through a game he made."

"*Voise*?"

I nod and show him the black key. "Why did the game teleport me here? Shouldn't the secret base be—secret?"

"That's an experiment he made." The blond sits beside me. "When players reach the True End, they're teleported here and automatically linked to him through a program in the key. In other words, anyone who wants to see him can see him—or even *touch* him. Of course, this experiment is illegal, so he had to carry it out under water."

I stare at the key. What the hell did Senso cigs do to Brother? How did he even come up with this idea? What else could he expect but the malice of strangers?

"What—what's the goal of this experiment?"

"He said he wanted to 'feel his own existence.'"

"And the result so far?"

The young man shakes his head and smiles. "If anything came of it . . . it's the album we're making."

"Tell me. How did you guys meet in the first place?"

Jonny straightens up. "That was years ago, when I had entered Sand Tower. My classmates dragged me to a show. I wasn't interested until I saw Azure from the band Polar Day. He was a nobody, just a game artisan dabbling in music, or so they said. But there he was, guitar in hand, programs floating around him, standing alone on the stage like a king. The music flowing from his hands was magical . . .

"I was still staring at him after everyone else had left. He fiddled with his guitar and asked, 'You like it?'

"I couldn't speak. He put the guitar in my arms and urged me to try. But I majored in music generation and had no idea how to play an antique instrument. Not to mention the guitar looked so *real* and expensive . . . He watched me struggle, then suddenly decided to give it to me.

"'No matter how *real* it seems, it's just a duplicate,' he said. 'But in your hands, it looks . . . more alive . . . '

"He taught me the basic chords, how to *feel* the guitar and my hands . . .

"I practiced guitar night and day, hoping to be worthy of that gift. I listened to every song he wrote, went to every show he performed—until he disappeared, leaving me a lost soul. No, there was no substitute for him. Then, six months ago, I heard about a game under water, one whose style and music felt so him. So I visited the Black Pearl.

"Rumor had it, if you reached the True End, you could meet the game artisan in person. And then here I was, sitting on this bench, watching a man in a white shirt approach . . .

"He said he was Weilan Yu and welcomed me. He'd met many guests: some wanted to hurt him, some feared being hurt, some wanted something from him, and some just wanted to keep their distance. Still, he was grateful to all these brief encounters."

"And you?" I ask, cupping my chin. "What did you want?"

Jonny bites his lip and smiles shyly. "I couldn't think straight—I was sweating. Finally, I took out the guitar and played a tune. It was a song I wrote myself, just a crude imitation, but when I finished, he exclaimed, 'See? It truly comes alive in your hands!'

"So I shamelessly asked, 'Please, let me stay and make music with you!!'"

And my brother even agreed. He truly has changed.

"And you've been making an album for six months?" I ask.

"Yeah," Jonny rises. "Come with me."

The sea on the wall parts, revealing a room behind it. For a brief moment, I believe the man I'm searching for is right here, as a familiar scent of paper, wood, rain, and tenderness fills the air. But he's not.

The room is softly lit, its wooden floor scattered with musical instruments I've never seen before. Jonny explains, "Weilan said, 'Let's make some new music!' So we collected all kinds of antique instruments, many I've never heard of. This is a violin. This is a Chinese flute . . . And look at this. It's a synthesizer from twenty years ago—fantastic, isn't it?"

Digital documents lie scattered on the floor—fragments of sounds and words, works that might have grown into masterpieces.

"How many pieces have you made so far?" I ask.

Jonny touches his neck, looking embarrassed. "We spent too much time experimenting . . . Only three. Weilan hasn't finished adjusting them yet, but to me, they're already magnificent. I promise—you've never heard anything like them. They're even different from his past works . . . "

"How were his past works?" I ask.

He stares at me, wide-eyed.

"You've never listened? After all these years? But—but he's your brother!"

"They . . . They're too avant-garde for my ears," I mumble.

At the end of the room sits an electric guitar, its wood grain deep and rich. A digital replica of Brother's beloved guitar—the one our parents smashed in a fight when he was a boy. Reborn here in the city of Laputa, it has become another boy's treasure.

I reach out, grazing its silky surface. I know—I always know. Brother's music isn't too avant-garde; it's just too heavy. His heart is too heavy for this city. Tied to it, I can't fly either.

"Jonny . . . " I plead, "Let me hear it. Let me hear your music."

There are no visuals, sensations, or interactions to guarantee a pleasant journey. Only sound, and Jonny, plucking at the strings. A few chords send sparks down my spine; I see a colorful, chaotic world, like a crumbling palace. I see a lost soul, staggering under the sun. Distortions glare, the melody sways. How could we escape this desolate earth and reach for the sky? Drums pound in reply, noises surge through my body, a treble note slices my skin. The strings break free, soaring past the wall of sound into heaven.

Heaven is cold and bright. A chant for pleasure hovers above hollow sound waves. Heaven's serenity besieges and smothers the melody; it struggles but finally rests in peace. Yet beneath it all, there's a noise—a glitch, a howl, a dark smear in this blinding radiance. A heart awakens, frosted, naked, trembling.

Blood breaks free from the ice, surging through thawing veins. The heart pounds again, like a beast battering its cage. The guitar line bursts forth like a little boy, staggering, stumbling, running with all his might. Legs quiver, heart pounds like thunder; he tumbles and bleeds but keeps running. Blood mingles with tears, merging into blazing blue before falling into blinding black.

A hand flashes across the strings; sweat flickers on the skin; Jonny bends lower and lower, as if the roaring guitar has become an unbearable weight. Lightning splits the darkness; fireworks explode before my eyes. What's the guitar crying for? What's it chasing? Something we lost long ago, something we cannot name—something we look at but cannot see. It's so beautiful, it hurts.

The boy can't run farther but crawls forward. Sound soars and explodes into a cloud. Lights pierce his eyes like gunfire; he rises, embracing the bullets.

Waves ebb and flow. Drizzles sweep across my skin. Piano notes approach softly, and I catch a familiar scent. It's Brother at twenty-three, smiling at me; at sixteen, holding my trembling hand; at ten, weeping silently by the river. I hear a familiar voice reciting a poem. A piano key falls, and a fading blue pulses its last heartbeat.

After the final note, polar lights rise.

Jonny is breathless, sweat dripping from his chin. His hands tremble—hard to believe they were just burning on the strings. He gapes at me through damp hair, and I find myself sitting on the floor, something cold on my face.

Tears. Staring at the liquid on my fingertip, feeling the ache in my chest, for the first time in years, I taste my true feelings.

"I thought I loved him," I whisper, "but I only love myself. But you, Jonny—aren't you afraid, daring to love someone?"

Jonny cradles his guitar. "Weilan asked me the same thing. He said I'd be free once we finished the album, that people like me were a miracle today, that he couldn't repay me and feared hurting me. He asked if I was afraid."

"And your answer?"

"I wasn't. I was happy," the blond replies with a serene smile.

I stand up and snap my fingers, rebooting my virtual body. "But he left you. Didn't even finish the album. Didn't even say goodbye."

Jonny reboots his body and sets the guitar down gently. "No, he said goodbye. Held my hands, told me he was grateful but had to leave and search for a 'ghost.' He gave me a coin, told me, 'This is for you. If someone ever comes for me . . . well, never mind,' and then disappeared."

Ghost. The word rings a bell.

Jonny takes out a transparent cube with a coin frozen inside. He removes the coin and places it in my palm. I gasp.

A GhostCoin. It resembles the coins we studied in history class, but it's as clear as ice. Engraved on its surface is Da Vinci's *Vitruvian Man*—a nude figure extending four arms and four legs. Unmonitored by Logos, GhostCoins seem to be a popular currency under water. I saw its rate at the bar: a small amount costs a fortune. And a whole coin like this means—

"Do you know how much it's worth?" I ask.

"I know," Jonny replies. "We could do twenty gigs with it."

"Putting aside how my brother got it, why not cash it in for Value Points and stop grinding through newbie tasks?"

"I don't want to." He turns away. "To be honest, I wasn't happy to get this coin. Felt like I did everything just for it."

See? He was hurt.

I fiddle with the coin. It's cold and weightless, like mist. Light passes through it, dancing on the Vitruvian. I suggest, "Brother said he met 'a ghost' six months ago, then went searching for it two weeks ago. Do you think by 'ghost,' he meant GhostCoins?"

Jonny shakes his head. "You think Weilan cares about things like that? No, I think he went looking for the coin's inventor. They say this person created many things, including Atlantis itself. But I can't even find out their name . . . "

"Atlantis?"

"The underwater world. When it was first built, they say it was far more prosperous and interesting than it is today."

Jonny touches the wall, turning it transparent. Outside in the dim waters, buildings and ruins waver like ghost ships. In the deep darkness, something sparks, then vanishes, pursued by a swarm of golden lights.

"Those are the antivirus programs of Logos," Jonny explains. "They destroy everything they find."

I cling to the glass wall, staring at this world of debris. It's far more dangerous than I imagined. I glance at the crystal-clear coin, wondering if I'll ever find my brother now that he's befriended a ghost.

In the dim light, the Vitruvian looks even eerier. The Vitruvian, his four hands reaching for the sky . . .

"Hands! Hands!" I shout, jumping to my feet.

"What hands?" Jonny asks, confused.

"How do I run a search here?" I try to grab his shoulders, only to disrupt his virtual form.

Atlanpedia shut down long ago. The search engine barely works here. Finally, I find an image of Da Vinci's *Vitruvian Man*, exactly mirrored in GhostCoin's design. But there's a slight difference—the Vitruvian on the coin points in different directions with his limbs.

"This coin isn't just valuable—" I exclaim. "As Brother said, 'if someone ever comes for me'—it's his signpost!"

"Coordinates," Jonny murmurs, staring at the coin. "It's giving the coordinates to somewhere much deeper under water . . . "

"Are you afraid?" I ask.

"Not even possible," the blond mutters, biting his lip.

The alarm clock rings; it's time to return to the sober dream of reality. Jonny puts the coin back.

"Go home. And don't come back. Weilan wouldn't want his sister in danger."

I glare at him, as if glaring at myself. "Sister? I don't even qualify as his sister. I'm an idiot, not even aware of what I've lost. You'll wait for me tomorrow, won't you?"

"Jonny!"

The blond crouches on the floor, peering through his fringe at a cloud of web pages. His eyes light up when he spots me.

"Miss Lazuli! I thought you weren't coming."

"Just Lazuli," I correct him, waving a pair of neon-green fighter gloves. "Managed to get them out of the lab—better than fighting empty-handed."

To study the sensation of pain, I spent some time in Solar Arena and did pretty well with these gloves. After that, I applied to bring them into the lab, preserving their power and one crucial feature: the ability to *touch* someone without permission. I demonstrate by grabbing Jonny's collar and effortlessly lifting him. He nearly panics.

"Come on," I say, letting go. "People down there are way scarier."

Scarier indeed. I have no idea where this trip will take us. What can we do against pirates, hackers, antivirus programs, and other fatal traps? "Anyway, I'm not abandoning my brother this time," I murmur.

Jonny shows me his research. "The Vitruvian on the coin points to three directions different from those in the painting. These three digits make up six coordinates, four are under water. Only one is valid, and that place is—" he pushes a web page toward me.

The notorious House of Mirth.

You won't find it in Lapupedia, of course. But even I know it's the largest underwater market, the source of Senso cigs and countless shady goods. They say you can buy any pleasure you want there—but whether you'll get scammed, hacked, bankrupted, or even erased depends on sheer luck.

"Well, let's check it out," I say. We put on our hoods, becoming two phantoms.

A dim void stretches before us. Glitter shimmers in the air like snake scales as a neon mandala blooms in the distance, red lips glowing at its center. Human figures appear beside us, darting toward it like mayflies. A neon tongue flicks, licking the lips, and the mouth snaps open, swallowing the flock.

I start to follow, but Jonny stops me. "Wait."

A golden light erupts, shattering the crowd. Figures vanish in bursts of teleportation or golden laser fire. A golden machine charges its laser—beep! A black hole forms on the lips, fuming with scattered pixels. The mouth bares its fangs and lunges—crunch, crunch! The sound of metal rending clatters through the darkness.

We drift toward the mandala, weaving through raincoat fragments and the wreckage of virtual forms.

"What happens to those attacked by antivirus programs?" I ask.

"Their affected data gets formatted. In the worst case, they have to abandon their ID."

We spot the remains of the machine, once a golden pyramid.

"We call them 'pyramid soldiers,'" Jonny says. "They've been multiplying lately, so firewalls have been reinforced everywhere."

The neon mouth gapes to welcome us. Its upper lip glows: "HOUSE OF MIRTH 3.0." The lower reads: "Resurrected only for your pleasure!"

We fly inside.

We stand amidst a kaleidoscope of ads. They spin, zoom, and shift, filling every inch of my vision as shadowy visitors swarm in every direction. Senso cigs, in every brand, intensity, and flavor, are just the mildest distraction. A few steps farther, and you'll see Senso Baths, Senso Whips, Senso Daggers, and Senso Bombs—all promising a rapid ride to White Eden. Weapons of every kind: anti-user, anti-corporation, anti-space, anti-service . . . Any object of desire: slaves, masters, lovers, family, strangers . . .

We step into an ad and fall into the body of a stranger, sharing her senses, peeping into her life. We step out and into another ad, where you can have yourself "killed" and "die" in painful ecstasy, only to wake up with your body rebooted, as if nothing happened. You can even live stream it, making good money for both "the victim" and "the killer." I feel sick, want to throw up—but I can't, because I'm just as hollow inside as these people.

Jonny reaches out as if to pat me but pulls back. "How about we look around for clues?" he suggests softly.

A search for "GhostCoin" takes us to Financial Harbor, where gold coins pave the streets and ads burst like fireworks. Colossal banks float in the sky, their signs suspicious. A search for "ghost" leads us to Uncanny Alley, where apparitions loom in the fog, offering secret cults, cyber curses, and urban legends. This isn't good—we're just wasting time here.

Jonny stares at the cube holding his coin, but I quickly hide it. "Careful not to be seen!"

"Don't worry. No one can take the coin from the cube without my key."

"What if you get scammed? Or it gets stolen?"

He pouts, ready to put the cube back, but I stop him. "Wait a second."

The coin gleams in the dark. I grab the cube and step deeper into the alley.

"This way," I whisper.

Everything in the House of Mirth is interconnected. Goods lead to shops, shops to ads, ads to spaces, ad infinitum. I cover the cube with my hands, following its guide as it brightens when we turn in the right direction. We rush past games and videos, heads down, for even a glance could drive us mad. We move through fine restaurants where beautiful men and women savor unimaginable things. We pass a clinic where unconscious bodies are linked to hacking programs, ready to be overwritten and pushed to overdrive. Hungry crowds devour fresh information—the more lurid, the better; no different from what's above water. Desires grow, distort, and form an unending maze, an unstoppable machine I was once part of.

The coin dazzles as we reach the edge of the House. This desolate area is likely the House of Mirth 1.0—or even 0.1. The buildings look as though they've been bombarded, with Roman columns collapsed and walls patched with glitches. We step into a gallery, a faint echo of Atlantis' glorious past. A bookstore boasts "perfect replicas of print books," yet its books lie scattered like trash. Few games remain in the game shop; the rest have crumbled into dunes of quicksand. Perfume, once an exquisite art, has become the olfactory mess left in the perfumery. Outside, colorful rain spatters from the night sky.

"Someone's following us," Jonny whispers.

We march on, Jonny stowing the cube as I maximize the gloves' output. Beyond the gallery is a semicircular square, where colorful rain puddles fade under the work of repair programs. Beyond the square's railings lies a void—or rather, a primordial soup of data. By the railings stands a strange device, even stranger as it appears untouched by the rain.

We take a turn and hide behind the walls.

A flash. A blast. Smoke rolls out. We dive to the side and look back at the wall, now a flickering phantom of green source code. A man emerges from the smoke, gun in hand—a powerful hacking gun I just saw in an ad.

I shove Jonny aside and leap at the gunman, landing a punch square on his face. His bones crackle as he's sent flying onto the square, splashing through colorful puddles. The gun slips from his grip and spins away.

I charge again, ready to land another blow, but he's already rebooted his body and kicks me hard in the stomach. Clearly, he's also equipped with something shady.

Blacked out, I tumble into a puddle, quicksand spilling into my eyes. Snapping my fingers to reboot, I spot a figure approaching—Jonny, aiming the gun at the man.

Whizz! The man ducks as an electric blast shatters the building behind him. He lunges at Jonny, pummeling him brutally, trying to seize the gun. Rolling to dodge the blows, Jonny flings the gun with all his strength—it skids over the railings.

The man scrambles after it, but I slam into him—

Shoving him into the void.

The void ripples, then stills. Only the sound of rain remains. Jonny lies face down, bruised and bleeding.

"Come on, reboot yourself!" I urge in a whisper.

He smiles weakly, unable to move a finger.

I help him sit up. He gasps for a moment before finally rebooting. "Sorry you had to touch me," he murmurs.

"Don't be silly," I reply.

"Where's the guy?"

I nod toward the void. "Taking a quicksand bath before Logos finds him." Then I recall an ad for Senso Bath—"Damn! He's probably enjoying it."

We approach the device by the railings. A tall stand holds a metallic tube with two holes; seems like we're supposed to look through them, but all I see is darkness. Stepping back, I notice floating words:

SCENIC TELESCOPE. Insert one coin.

"What's a telescope?" I ask Jonny. He shakes his head.

"Is there even any scenery to see?" I mutter, finding the coin slot on the stand. Jonny pulls out his coin, now gleaming like a full moon. It fits perfectly.

"Are you sure you want to use it?" I warn him. "You're giving away your last Value Points."

He smiles. "At this point, what's their value to me?"

The coin tinkles down the slot. Nothing happens, and the hairs on my neck start to rise. Jonny presses his eyes to the viewing holes and—

He turns into an arc of light. Reaching for him, I'm pulled in as well.

A room. Empty except for a table, a chair, and a bookshelf. Sunset pours through the panoramic windows, a beach stretches outside, waves echo. A man stands by the windows.

"Brother—" I start but hold my tongue.

This man is taller, his hair lighter. No raincoat—just a sweater and an overcoat. Brother could shift his appearance, of course, but something tells me this isn't the man I'm looking for.

I march forward. The wooden floor feels like it's made of marshmallow. The chair is too soft, the table too cold. The room stretches endlessly, while the sea looks impossibly far. Like a dream-space.

The man turns. He must be in his forties—I've never seen anyone this old in Laputa. His face is stern, his hair gray, and his eyes a frosty blue. But when he smiles, all those sharp features soften in the dusk.

"Here you are," he looks at us, or no one in particular. "Thanks for still remembering me."

He gazes at the landscape. "I have to leave now; sorry I can't say goodbye to you in person. I just can't hide anymore. The only thing I can do for this city is finish off the monster I created, even if it means chasing it to the world's end. If I haven't returned by the time you're watching this video, you can enter this door and follow the road. Whatever I find, I'll hide it there."

A window glows, transforming into a door to the sea. The sun radiates its last rays, and the waves crash against the shore with a horrible reverberation.

"It's not an easy path. I've set up defenses and weapons, but there's no guarantee for your safety. You can turn back anytime and return to your old life. Anyway, thank you for searching for the answer with me—it makes a ghost feel a little alive. You know, it's all too easy for a ghost to dissolve into simple digits, or simple desire . . . "

He raises a hand to shield his eyes from the sunlight.

"Well. I didn't know I missed this sea by my home so much . . . "

"Take care, and goodbye."

The dusk blurs his smile, and he steps into the afterglow. Only the sound of waves lingers in the room.

I turn to Jonny. "Do you think he's . . . "

"The ghost." Jonny nods. "But what happened to him? And what's this 'monster'?"

As if in response, translucent text appears in the air, glinting in the sunlight. Long or short, signed or unsigned, they're messages left by past visitors. I spot an anonymous message and recognize its handwriting at once. Jonny reaches for it, only to pass through wavering light.

You probably didn't get the coin from Ghost himself. Before making your choice, you need to know who he is. It was he who founded Logos seventeen years ago and ultimately created Laputa. It was also he who, three years ago, called upon people to go under water and build Atlantis. Logos destroyed Atlantis and sought revenge on him, accidentally severing the connection between his mind and body, leaving him a ghost in truth.

But why did he turn against his own creation? He said he regretted making it. Laputa was no longer the city he once dreamed of; it had become as desolate as the surface of the moon. So he began searching for an answer, even after becoming a ghost. How else could he live on?

At that moment, I found the question I had been searching for. And now, I'll follow this road. If you've followed me all the way down here . . . I'm sorry. I hope we meet again.

"*Goodbye.*" "*I'll follow!*" "*So this is Ghost.*" "*Can't understand him.*" Messages spark and sway, a silent cacophony. I read them, my mind utterly empty. Ahead waits Brother, beyond the door and that shining sea. Behind stands another door, leading back to where we came from—a white void.

A message gleams in the corner: "The sea is frightening."

The sea is frightening. The words slip down my throat, icy and sharp, summoning distant memories. But Jonny steps forward calmly, merging into the dusk. I rush after and grab his arm.

Codes rain down, pulling us into a whirlpool of colors. As our vision clears, we find ourselves standing on glowing concentric hexagons within a circle. Deep in the dim ocean, dunes of quicksand engulf archways and staircases. In the distance, the ruins of a white building shimmer, its structure formed of concentric hexagons as well. No one's here, not even a pyramid soldier. Only silence.

With a flying leap, we pass through the gate at the heart of the hexagonal ruins.

We emerge in a hexagonal room. Dark and spacious, it's entirely made of glass, revealing the deep sea beyond. Six glass walls enclose us: one opens into a passageway, while the other five are lined with shelves stretching from floor to ceiling. They display trinkets of all kinds, all of the same size: a toy dinosaur, a board game, a shirt, a necklace, something like a bracelet but showing time, something metallic to write with, books, photos, an apartment, a piano, a seashell, a withered flower, or nothing but a lingering scent.

I dare not make a sound, as if peering into the secrets of others or disturbing those at rest. In a whisper, I ask Jonny, "What is this place?"

The blond seems lost in thought. "Babel . . . The Museum of Babel!"

"Museum?" The word stirs a vague memory. Damn, I can't even run a search here.

"Museums preserve samples of vanished things," he explains. "When people first moved to Laputa, their bandwidths were limited, so they could only bring their body data. Someone built this museum, letting everyone scan one thing to keep here as a souvenir. Weilan said he 'borrowed' a few musical instruments from here . . . "

I sift through my memory. Either I never heard of this museum, or I didn't have anything worth preserving. "What did my brother keep here?"

Jonny shakes his head, smiling faintly. "He didn't tell me."

Could it be that replica of his guitar? But he gave it away so easily. Perhaps he hadn't kept anything here, tired of that old reality. I walk past the collections, my fingers trailing along the glass shelves, leaving glowing, fleeting traces. The display shifts for me, revealing objects that feel oddly familiar: antique game consoles, vintage clothes, faces known and unknown, and . . . a book I know too well.

I take it down with trembling hands. It's *the* book—I recognize its rough and yellowed pages at once. I turn to the page with the poem "Rain." Beneath the pencil lines Brother had jotted, my doodles spread—so big and ugly they hurt my eyes.

I was just a kid, and my brother a teenager. He had traded his valuables for this edition of *Borges: Selected Poems* and loved it, but my doodles soon ruined it. He couldn't bring himself to yell at me or fight me, so he just stopped talking to me for a month. I felt lucky to have gotten off easy: printed books were relics, and how could I ever find another copy? We never mentioned the book again.

But here it is, with the same look, texture, and ugly doodles. Why didn't Brother erase them from this digital replica? Even I could do that easily. And what do they depict?

In the drizzles, a boy and a girl stand by the sea, hand in hand.

It was Brother and me.

I press my forehead to the book, breathing in the scent of old paper. Jonny watches me silently, some sheet music in his hand. I carefully put the book back and look toward the passageway.

"Will Mr. Ghost show us the way?" I tease, "he won't love seeing us grope around and waste time, right?"

Jonny steps into the passageway, crossing an invisible gate shimmering with code. The next moment, the corridor crackles and reshapes, the labyrinth itself paving the way for us. We pass through countless rooms, identical except for their collections. Each time we enter a new passageway, the space ahead remodels. We start running, the collections blurring into phantoms: a cat, a pair of shoes, a building brick . . . reminding me of a digital paradise.

Suddenly, I stumbled over something—a splash of golden quicksand, where a broken machine lies buried.

"A pyramid soldier!" I leap back.

Jonny crouches to examine it. "It's not the usual model. See those patterns? This might be an advanced one."

"Did it follow us all the way down here?"

"Or was it drawn here by the visitors before us?" He sighs. "Thank goodness Ghost had left strong defenses."

Looking at the wreck of the golden machine, I shudder to think what would've happened if it had hit—or worse, caught—me. I remember the glinting messages in Ghost's room: how many of the visitors have taken this path? And how many have persisted? Well, at least they have some kind of tech, or guts. Do I even have the courage to face a pyramid soldier?

Speaking of the devil—

We duck behind a shelf, holding our breath as a pyramid soldier cruises through the next room. It buzzes and beams, slowly eroded by the firewalls.

We exchange helpless looks. Should we stay hidden? It could detect us any second. Should we run? This time, I don't want to run away again. Besides, we'd have to run all the way back on foot since teleporting doesn't work here. My hands sweat—where are the weapons Ghost left for us?

Like moonbeams, silver source code rises from our palms. An icon appears in the air: a hand miming shooting and punching.

Uh-oh. Worst game ever—one life, no reload.

Jonny mimics a shooting gesture, silver light gathering at his fingertip. Holding his breath, gritting his teeth, he aims—and bang!

Quicksand pours down, and a golden mist rolls out. The soldier lies buried in the sand, its surface still shiny. It hasn't been here long—it followed us all the way down. And there'll be more of them.

"Hooah, you're a sniper!" I praise Jonny, trying to play it cool. "Are you an expert at shooter games?"

"My first time playing," he replies, his ears turning red.

I kick the wreck, and we head toward the next passageway. Suddenly, a golden light flashes—"Watch out!" Jonny shouts.

The wreck rises, reforming into two small pyramids that blast laser beams. Jonny shoves me aside just as they hit the shelves, sending a rain of glass and a glitching black hole marked "NO DATA."

I fire at the pyramids, only to shatter more glass. Jonny shoots, taking one down. The other darts toward me—I swing a punch, but it ducks. It dodges and flees into the last room. We follow but lose its trail.

"Well, we let go of a problem," I gasp, rebooting my body.

"We have to speed up," Jonny says.

We race through rooms and passageways, past wrecks of golden machines, until we arrive at a room where the entrance vanishes as we step inside. It holds a similar collection, except for a peculiar paper craft: a paper model of LAPUTA.

Two cones are glued together back-to-back. The upper cone depicts the city I know, adorned with landmarks like Logos Tower, crafted from candy wrappers, and Sand Tower, made from cardboard. The lower cone, inverted, is divided into three sections labeled "WEB 3.0," "2.0," and "1.0," with a zero at its pointed tip. I'm stumped.

Jonny examines the model and presses its midpoint. It cracks open like a treasure chest, releasing a file fragment and a dozen messages. I recognize Brother's:

I'm not surprised Ghost chose the museum as his fortress. After all, we've all entrusted something important here. Not to mention, this museum was built by Ghost himself. He said people needed a place to store their memories of Earth, for they would soon be forgotten.

Indeed. After a few months, no one came to preserve anything. Within a few years, the museum itself was forgotten. Laputa became a city without memory, and its residents became weightless. Where will we drift?

I copy the fragment and glance at the other messages: the journey was horrifying, the travelers were afraid, but they kept on. A light glimmers in the paper model, leading to somewhere unknown.

"Ready?" I ask Jonny.

"Can't wait," he replies. We leap toward the light.

Phantom faces gleam in the dark—my face, in fact, reflected in black mirrors: square, rectangular, and eyeglass-shaped, whole or shattered. I step back, treading on glass shards. Black shards form rivers and mountains, while black mirrors shape the sky. Quicksand pours down from the cracks in the sky, forming shining pillars and clotting like lava. Luckily, no pyramid soldiers in sight.

"What the heck is this place?" I murmur.

Jonny touches a mirror. It lights up, displaying garish icons with cheap texture and outdated designs. He taps a random icon, and the display shifts: a pretty girl dances in retro clothes—or perhaps not retro. Just ancient.

"Black Mirror. The Era of Black Mirror," Jonny exclaims.

"As my brother mentioned?"

Jonny nods. "It was the era when we were kids, or even before we were born. Back then, there was no Laputa, not even Vision Glasses.

People accessed the Internet through 'black mirrors.' They stared into them night and day, yearning to enter the world within. Sadly, it was impossible, as the Internet was still two-dimensional."

"How pathetic," I remark, suddenly struck by a thought—how will people in the future view us? Will they pity us too?

We light up mirror after mirror, searching for a signpost. Cheerful music, harsh laughter, alluring goods, overwhelming information . . . Not much different from our time. We travel along glass rivers, encountering ghostly faces, many no longer among the living. As the urban legends go, pieces of their souls were captured and trapped in this two-dimensional world, this dreamland and digital landfill . . .

The lights go out, leaving only our reflections in the mirrors. Suddenly, they begin to march on their own, and we follow suit. We tread through mountains and valleys of glass, crossing rivers and streams of quicksand. At some point, a big white dog joins our reflections, running happily ahead.

The three of them stop at a glade, where black mirrors scatter like gravestones, and a pillar of quicksand cascades in silence. I crouch down, plunging a hand into the sand. Information floods my mind—sounds, scents, colors, emotions . . . I shake my head to force them away.

We start digging as a golden shadow slides by.

I drag Jonny behind a mirror, which then shatters into a thousand pieces. We run as laser beams scorch everything in our wake, creating black holes of NO DATA. Ahead, two pyramids emerge, linked by glowing tubes to a broken machine—the one we had let go.

"Cover me!" I cry.

Jonny nods, shouting, "Remember, they can split!"

He fires just as I dash out. One pyramid crumbles, and I land a punch to finish it off. I leap at the others, but they dodge and fly toward Jonny, unleashing infernal fires. Jonny fires moonbeams from behind a mirror, taking down an enemy. But it soon rises—then splits in two. Beams, explosions, and then the boy falls silent.

I take a deep breath, aiming at the host pyramid.

Boom! The host drifts down, its tubes burning out. The others begin to twitch as I dash, fire, and take cover from the explosion.

Darkness falls. Colorful sand sprinkles down onto a motionless body. Jonny lies on the ground, his coat shredded, his body rebooted. Yet black scars of NO DATA still spread across him, especially over his eyes.

Our reflections and the dog watch us silently from the mirrors.

"Got them?" Jonny gazes at the dim sky with blind eyes.

"No. They got away."

He lets out a sigh. "You did your best. Just dig out the fragment and go ahead; I'll catch up later."

I help him up, leading him forward, hand in hand.

"What're you doing?" he protests. "I said, leave me here!"

"Aren't you the most eager to meet Brother again?" I counter. "I won't let you run away now. And don't ever think I'll leave you to those sharks."

He falls silent.

We stagger over glass shards and shining icons. Jonny bumps into a mirror, and a face of NO DATA leaps out, grinning at us. I grip his arm, feeling the texture and warmth of his virtual skin. " . . . Otherwise, it would all be meaningless," I murmur.

"Why?" he asks softly.

I shake my head.

"That day, Brother's guitar was smashed. We hid in our room, listening to our parents fight. Brother held me so tightly it hurt, but I knew he was hurting even more.

"'There's a place,' he said, 'where you can piece back anything broken. A place where everyone will be whole . . . '

"But he was wrong. Laputa deceived us, just like these mirrors deceived their owners. People believed they would be complete and happy if they could enter the world within. Indeed, we've become as whole as these mirrors, as these sands . . . "

I guide Jonny's hand into the sand. We start digging again, information rushing and fading in our minds.

"So I can't leave you here," I murmur. "Otherwise, it would all be meaningless—for me and for him . . . "

I feel something smooth and cold: a small black mirror. It lights up, displaying a big white dog—the one we just saw, but much older. The date reads twenty years ago.

I reach for the dog, only to touch cold glass. A file fragment rises, along with a few messages. Brother said:

The Museum of Babel preserves people's memories, but who will preserve the world's? Ghost once led me deep under water to a larger museum he built. When he first designed Laputa, he left room in the city's reflection to preserve the past of the Internet.

Archaeologists read the names of time from strata. I, too, named the eras of Laputa. Ours is the Era of Cellophane; here was the Era of Black Mirror, and before that, the Era of Inscription. This larger museum preserves not only the world's memories but also a piece of its soul.

We reach out to the light, to a piece of the world's soul.

• • •

Somewhere even deeper, the place itself is a crystallization of time. Rectangles stretch beneath our feet, large and small, layer upon layer, framed in gray and adorned with buttons. Inside, bright text glows against colorful backgrounds, tacky cartoons bounce about, and music blares from every direction.

"What's that sound?" Jonny asks. "What do you see?"

"An ancient relic," I reply, describing the scene for him. "Honestly, they could've used a bit more taste."

I lead him across the rectangles. When we step on underlined text, the content beneath our feet vanishes, replaced by massive warning signs such as 404 and 502. Sometimes, we disappear ourselves, teleported to another rectangle.

"Brother once said books were the predecessor of the Internet," I recall. "The early Internet was like those printed books, compiled page after page. He must have been describing this era."

"Even Ghost probably wasn't born yet," Jonny muses.

We search for a signpost. Looking closer, these "web pages" aren't so bad. Behind each one is a real person, introducing themselves to the world, sharing their lives and thoughts like children sharing their treasures. Emails are scattered everywhere, unbelievably long; it shocks me how much they had to say to one another back then. Back then, the Internet was an open playground: without tech, without taste, people created a world so rich and colorful. Mostly, they earned nothing from it, not even a single Love Vote. Still, they poured their lives into it, willingly, with a foolish passion, as if—

"As if they were in love with this world," Jonny says.

In love—where did he learn such outdated words?

"Who's there?!" he cries, and I hold my breath. Beneath the sound of synthesizers, a faint noise draws near. Jonny points in a direction, and I see a white arrow shuffle by, stopping at an underlined text, waiting for us.

What the heck is that? I swallow the question.

"It's the only thing here that moves freely," I say. "Guess it served as people's virtual bodies back then."

How dowdy. I poke at the arrow, and it flits away, leaving a trail of shadows. We walk to the underlined text as the arrow morphs into a cartoon hand—and clicks.

We fall through the sediment of web pages. As we travel back in time, their appearances grow simpler. Music fades away, followed by animated cartoons and static images. Eventually, we find ourselves on an endless plain of black text against a white background.

"World Wide Web," a page reads.

We teleport from one underlined text to the next. "*A project that uses hypertext concepts . . . freely available to anyone . . .* " I read for Jonny, then explain, "So this is the first website ever built in this world."

"And the bottom of our world," Jonny adds.

Indeed. The strata of web pages above and the black-and-white plain below make up the entire world we know.

"Where is the arrow?" Jonny asks.

The arrow has vanished. The black-and-white plain flickers and fades, and we fall into an abyss of text.

This was the eve of the World Wide Web. It was barren, filled only with text. It was fertile, nurturing everything. Texts sprawled across the wilderness. Logs, long and short, formed thorny bushes. Sites bloomed into monochrome forests, colorful in essence. ASCII characters pieced together to depict a face from half a century ago. Brick by brick, a home was built: *Star Trek* discussions paved the floor; descending stairs led to MUD games; library catalogs formed towering columns, with NASA's launch history engraved at the top. Beside a little poem by an unknown poet, I spot something moving—a flickering dash.

"Guess the soldiers can't follow us this far down," Jonny says optimistically.

"Hopefully." I smile.

Arm in arm, we chase the dash. We march through the arches of FTP services, down the sub-boards of BBS. Murals glow along dark passageways, drawn only with characters: *Spaceships*, *Snoopy*, *Mona Lisa*, *Egyptian Gods* . . . fantastic, considering the tools they had.

"Why put so much effort into a single painting?" I wonder aloud. "I wouldn't have the patience to draw even a line like that."

"It's like drilling wood to make fire," Jonny comments, using yet another obsolete phrase.

The dash leads us farther down along the murals of *Nautilus*. On long nights like these, people overcame obstacles—high costs, complex operations, endless waiting, and the risk of system collapse—to reach this place. Here, the sky was new, and the earth still veiled in mist. They roamed the wilderness with their little lights, leaving footprints, seeking one another, and creating new worlds. Crying, laughing—these ordinary people and the faintest traces they left built a cathedral of our own.

We walk toward the light.

"What will you say when you meet Brother?" I ask Jonny.

He tenses. "I don't know . . . I once dreamed of it, but I couldn't say a word."

"And I," I gaze into the distance, the light radiating with a touch of blue, "I want to tell him I remembered that day . . . "

When I was little, I whined about wanting to see the sea, but our parents were too busy for a long trip. Then one day, out of the blue, they took us on a journey. We went to another city to see a river—the closest thing to the sea they could show me. Dad and Mom stood at a distance while Brother quietly strolled, and I ran around in the river park. When I returned, Brother was watching an old man writing Chinese calligraphy on the floor tiles with a huge brush and water.

I was too young to read any of them, but like Brother, I was captivated by the beautiful characters on the ground. Soon, though, they began to fade under the sun, making Brother anxious. The old man shook his head and said, "Never mind."

The sun blazed down, and more and more characters evaporated. Brother tugged at the old man's shirt and asked, "Why? Why write all these beautiful characters just to let them disappear?"

The old man paused, then smiled. "Because I've finished writing them," he said, before moving to another spot to start anew.

Brother stared at the fading characters, his hand frozen in the air. Then, in silence, he wept.

That was the last time my family went out together. A few years later, our parents got divorced. A few more years passed, and no one would marry. Sometimes, I recall the image of a ten-year-old boy gazing at a glittering river, tears streaming down his cheeks. What was reflected in his eyes? What was on his mind?

"On that day, I found my brother a stranger. Since then, I've never been able to understand him. But now, when I meet him, I'll tell him I've started to understand, little by little . . . "

The sky sparkles before our eyes. We descend a spiral staircase into a square hall, where black archways rise on each side, winds howling beyond them. Take another step, and you'll fall into the unfathomable sky.

I study the white text on the black walls, summing it up: "If I'm right, these are the first four nodes of humanity's first network—the ARPANET."

Jonny gasps in awe. "Can you find the file fragment?"

The flickering dash darts across the walls, guiding us toward one archway. Shielding my eyes from the dazzling sky, I scan the white text on the black floor, then spot a blue pixel. Next to it, half-buried in crystal sand, lies a broken smart choker.

I pick it up. Why is it here? It doesn't show NO DATA, so it wasn't damaged by the soldiers—then who? The smart choker syncs the user's body data. What happens when it breaks?

I prod the blue pixel. The final fragment rises, merging with the others and starting to parse. Three messages glow beside it: one says they'll quit and forget everything; one says they'd go to Atlantis to warn everyone—clearly, they didn't make it. The last is written in a familiar hand:

Go home.

Home? Where is home?

The file finishes parsing and reveals itself. Images swarm up, tattered and flickering. Documents are written in a strange style, as if not meant for humans. I try to interpret them for Jonny, "Two years ago, there was an experiment, probably successful . . . but soon the subject escaped. And then . . . it was decided that the experiment shall be conducted all across Laputa; anyone against it shall be erased. Wait, the escaped subject was—"

An unfamiliar name. A familiar face.

"Ghost," I whisper.

The first soul ever severed from its living body.

And soon, all souls in Laputa will follow.

Jonny shoves me aside before the floor explodes. Two sets of pyramids swoop down, each carrying a battered host and two shining satellites. I hide Jonny behind the debris and dash forward, smashing the leading enemy. Sand pours, rubble scatters, and beams fire, burning black trenches of NO DATA into the ground. I drag the boy to an archway as the rest of the pyramids emerge from the dust. I land a punch on one enemy, dodge the beams, and leap to finish another. Turning back, I see only a gripping hand on the archway—Jonny has climbed to the outside of the hall. What's out there but the endless sky?

I have no choice. Three laser beams are drawing near. Grasping the arch frame, I swing across to the outside.

A rock-gray wall stretches before me. A narrow path lies beneath my feet. Grabbing the protruding pixels on the wall, we tread carefully ahead, our hair whipped by the wind. An invisible firewall blocks the pyramids as we turn the corner and reach the next wall.

Rumble, crackle, bang! Two pyramids break through, now creaky and slow, yet still fatal. We hide behind the corner, waiting for the buzz to approach.

Smack! I land a blow just as a golden beam flashes.

Jonny shields me from the explosion. I stare at my hands—they've vanished, replaced by two black holes of NO DATA.

The buzzing fades as the last pyramid retreats for now. Silence falls over the howling wind.

"I'll cover you," Jonny says. "You take a detour to strike from behind."

I raise my broken arms. "I can't, Jonny. My hands are gone. I can't strike anymore . . . "

He falls silent.

"Lazuli," he says, calling my name for the first time. "Stay here. When you hear a noise, run upward as fast as you can."

He takes a stride, trying to move past me, only to disrupt my virtual form. Suddenly, I realize what he's doing and leap to stop him, but without my gloves, I can't even touch him. My broken arm passes right through him, flickering in vain.

"Jonny, DON'T!" I cry.

He pauses.

Neither of us speaks. The wind wails, the buzz grows near. My brain storms with questions. *Go home*—but how? By surrendering and abandoning our names, memories, or something even more essential, then snapping open our eyes to become brand new citizens? *Go home*—I glance at the dazzling sky, the eternal sun, the fleeting clouds, and the dark cyan ocean beneath. The Sea of Fertility—a place that also exists in reality. The youngest sea, named with irony. I raise my head to look at the blind young man, red data streaming through his choker like blood.

"Let's go home!" I shout. "Brother must have gone there too. Believe me, Jonny, and break our chokers!"

His face glows in the sunlight. He finds my choker with one hand and places the other on his own. Abandon our chokers; abandon our cyber blood; abandon our birthright in the greatest city of humanity. Sparks flare, and we fall toward the sea.

I wake from a dream. The room is white, its light soft, and its walls cushioned. My body feels like stone. Painstakingly, I move my fingers, grasping the tech fabric of the bedsheet. Slowly, I sit up. Tubes and wires slip free, the smart choker falling to the floor. Dull and unresponsive, it's just a broken toy now.

I brace myself against the bedside. The food, fitness, and sanitation modules remain embedded in the floor, unresponsive now that they no longer detect my presence. For eight hours a day, I eat, exercise, clean, and slip into dreamless sleep, all alone in this ninety-square-foot room. Like everyone else, I never once felt the need to leave.

Today, for the first time in years, I step out barefoot.

An endless white corridor stretches ahead, lined with identical white doors. Each has no name, no number—only a white-or-gold indicator light. All of them glow gold now, signaling the person inside is in the virtual dream. My light has gone dark, as I'm no longer a citizen of Laputa. All these lights may soon fade, should these people no longer be habitants of Earth.

The floor glows faintly, cold beneath my feet. The corridors twist and intersect like a labyrinth. At a crossroads, I meet a nurse bot, which simply ignores me.

Mingling with silent robots, I descend a massive escalator. After all these years, I see the full expanse of this egg-shaped facility once more. Soft light sprinkles through its translucent dome, illuminating layer upon layer of white rooms and a vast, empty hall. I cross it, passing two rows of unseeing security bots.

On the mountaintop, scorching winds lash my delicate skin. Below lies a deserted city, its metal and glass gleaming in the sun, wavering in the heat. I walk down the hill, leaving Facility No. 078215 behind. Tech fabric can't handle the heat; sweat streams down my spine, soaking my back in salt. Treading the boiling asphalt, my feet begin to burn.

Before they bleed, I find a pair of shoes in an abandoned home. I fill a backpack at an unattended supermarket. In the suburbs, I spot the transport station, where a driverless bus carries me through the empty streets. A black cat leaps from the sidewalk; a human figure flickers around the corner. They say some people chose to stay, and so they did, cared for by robots.

The auto-train departs, and the city fades into a phantom. Across the wilderness, I see no one but massive machines passing by. Finally, I step off the platform, returning to my hometown after a decade. Now, it has a sea.

Humid winds sweep through the streets. Years ago, people evacuated before the environmental catastrophe, leaving the city empty. Most never returned, after becoming proud new citizens of Laputa.

The driverless bus fails to reach its destination, so I trudge through the rubble, finding my way home by memory. I know, by instinct, that Brother will be there.

Home was devoured by the sea. In the afternoon light, the water gleams an aquatic blue, almost transparent. Beneath its sparkling surface, roads lie buried, colorful roofs loom, skyscraper peaks rise. Enveloped by the sound of waves, I smell the sea for the first time. Mellow, salty, rolling like a beast.

I write a message in the sand with my feet, watching the waves nibble at its edge. As the sky darkens, I walk across the ruins and find an apartment to rest in. The next day, someone waits for me by the sea.

Feet in the waves, pants rolled up, a young man gazes into the horizon. A bag and a guitar rest on his back, picked up from somewhere. He turns, his hair and freckles glowing in the sun, and smiles shyly.

I smile back. In reality, we look pale and exhausted. He's not as handsome, and I'm not as pretty. We both wear standard white clothes, now dirty and sticky. Sweat streaks our faces, and salt stains our backs.

"Ni hao, wo jiao Jonathan Wave," he says, his Chinese quite off.

I gather all the English I can. "My name is Qunqing Mu. It means . . . herding the color . . . ultramarine."

We reach for each other's hands. A small lightning flashes through our skin, and we pull back.

We spend two days searching and find Brother's trace in an unfinished building. As I climb the floors, I catch a full view of the sea through a concrete frame. In one room, tools and groceries are stacked; in another, books lie scattered. In the glow of the sea, beside a few books, I spot a broken drone and some dried blood. I pick up a bloodstained notebook, its cover burning with blue.

It's Brother's diary and poetry journal. I read aloud as I copy, through the afternoon and into the dusk. We light a fire by the sea, which turns out to be much harder than I imagined. The planks are too damp, and I'm too afraid to light the fire, so Jonny does. We feed page after page into the flames, watching the fire dance, and finally put in the whole notebook. The night sky is clear, the fire flares, and we sit, watching it burn.

My toes sink into the damp sand as a tiny crab scuttles past. The air cools; the tides rise and fall, leaving foam along the beach. The fire crackles in the dark, paper scraps flying through the air. The sky lights up with a dainty pink on the horizon, fading into soft turquoise. Seagulls glide by, and in the pale blue sky, a constellation of satellites rises—the future of humanity, continuing without us.

We stand hand in hand, gingerly, in fear of hurting each other. The sky turns azure, and a true life starts here.

Originally published in Chinese in *Science Fiction World*, May 2021.

Translated by the author.

ABOUT THE AUTHOR

Bella Han's works have appeared in *Clarkesworld, Science Fiction World,* the annual Best Chinese Science Fiction, and more. She was the winner of the China Galaxy Award and the Stellar Award. Based in Hangzhou, China, she is passionate about all forms of art.

Heart of Thunder

RAAHEM ALVI

Present

Damian Marshall was a prisoner to his own brain. He was beating his fist against the glass of his cell, hoping someone could hear that this was not the real him. It was never meant to be this way and, truthfully, he had a heart swelling with love to give.

Damian Marshall was not an evil man, but he was beginning to think that was a lie. No one quite sets out to be evil, he supposed. Malice was a byproduct of some evolutionary self-preserving mammalian instinct. Sometimes evil just happened without intention.

There are mistakes, then there are crimes. And it was difficult to determine the lines between these two forms of evil to definitively categorize his many actions in Ganymede Settler Colony.

"What happened in Ganymede, Mr. Marshall?"

He didn't know. He really didn't. His neural augmentations had fucked up the rest of his brain makeup.

"You were exploited. You just need to testify. We can save you from this."

Damian had always heard voices from his occipital bone. And he was beginning to hear new ones somewhere in the jelly consistency of his brain between all the gray matter. It was a failing neural implant buzzing and coiling inside, screeching, "failing, failing, failing."

"These were prototype military augmentations. You never should have received them. This is on them."

He needed someone to take a spear to his skull and calm the electric radiation of a failing augmentation. He needed someone to fix the cybernetics, their corrosive tissue melting into the meat of his organic form. He had given so much of himself to the Corporatocracy.

Where did he start, and where did the augmentations begin?

"Module is reassigning you to Mars Labor Colony 12. That place is privately owned by them. Once you're there, I can't help you."

The thing that identified as Damian Marshall was coiling in an ouroboros-like cycle somewhere within the recesses of his cyborg consciousness.

Maybe Damian was faultless because he wasn't quite there anymore.

Mars was an unwelcoming little corner of the universe. The freight ship entered through the stratosphere as a missile. And the hostile desert winds set upon it a full-frontal assault.

Damian Marshall was a broken man. But he knew, somewhere between his lungs and his spine, that being broken is just a neutral state for *Homo sapiens*. Age was slow degradation. Things are made finite for they, by nature, are meant to break. And breaking is all a part of intelligent, conscious design within the neural fields of the universe.

Everything had an end to it. Thus, things had to be exceedingly fragile. So, Damian concluded, his neurological health was one of the many things with a purposeful expiration. It just so happened that his mental health died before his body. So now he carried rot inside his skull. And the necrotic tissue of his sinking self-worth was smelling the innards of their freight ship.

"Grab your bags, grab your supplies, oxygen masks on—"

Damian Marshall was sad. But sadness happens to the best of us.

The problem is when sadness is deserved.

Metal panels collapsed from their place, and wires tossed out. Loose parts struck heads and masks. The gray, cramped chamber where they were belted down sent them into a frenzied maelstrom of rattling and screaming metal.

Damian closed his eyes and felt it drawing closer.

Yes. It. That Thing. The Thing that sends shivers up and down his spine in electric waveform particles, darting in zigzag motions into his neurons. That It—the It that evokes panic and fear in him. That It that still haunts the imprints of his footsteps in Ganymede.

Past

Memories are approximations. They are stretchy, squishy, and fluid things. And, as time stretches to its elastic limit, the mind begins filling certain subsections of time with fiction. And then it eternalizes those fictions as fact. Then fact and fiction fuck and grind against one another until they merge into a twin-headed zombie thing.

"Interview. Damian Samuel Marshall, age 23."

Damian stared at the lens of the camera, its black glassy exterior a bit judgmental of his rugged state.

"According to your medical records, you've always had hallucinations and delusions but no real diagnosis. Never got along well with teachers and classmates, nor did you perform that well in your school. Your resume is virtually empty, and you have no clear set of skills. So tell me Damian, why Module?"

Damian kept staring at the singular glassy black hole, its rim coiling and looping his consciousness within its circumference. He had learned a script for this moment. And he had been learning to mimic others and the tones and inflections in their voices. But as he tried forcing out the words from somewhere deep in his belly, a monstrous hazard inside him began swelling. And each attempt at speaking felt as if he were picking at it.

"I want to do something with my life," Damian replied.

"What does doing something mean, Damian?"

"Rationalizing my existence. Assign it some meaning, however temporary and inglorious, to get through my life."

"You don't find self-actualization from jobs, Damian."

Where else then? Damian wondered, knowing a vast majority of his life would be bound to employment contracts—one after another. Where else did self-actualization arise when life outside of employment was so brief and minuscule?

"I need something to fit in the picture to make it make sense because it looks so fucked up."

The anxieties of unemployment had wrapped inside him. Money was a part of the symptom. But most of it was the meandering erosion of his existence.

You see, Damian Marshall was becoming an alien to his own body. And there was nothing scarier than being trapped inside your own mortal shell by the machinations of your mind. It had become hostile to Damian and started killing him from the inside-out, which decayed him from the outside-in.

"Your brain is not cooperative with current augmentations. You can't hold any labor jobs because you lack physical enhancements. And no office jobs because you lack neural enhancements. You can't survive in the current job market with your organic form, Damian. Existence has moved past the animal kingdom. You need to catch up to the tech era."

Damian felt as if cutting and replacing parts of his organic body would take away what little control he had over it. But the pressure of hooking industry-standard enhancements and augmentations into him had grown over the years.

"We're beyond people like you, Damian. Tech built the world. And tech runs it, too. So, think again: what do you really want?"

Damian wanted someone to make it make sense. He wanted it to fit within the picture frame as a complete observable whole, rather than bits and pieces of scraps he had to fit together and hope that he did a good enough job of putting it all in place, like others did.

He felt alien.

A neurodivergent invader in the lives of "regular" people. This was a hostile planet where everyone reserved no place for him within the hierarchy. He was an observer, at society's feet, hoping to wash the fungus between its toes enough to slip through it.

"I want to feel normal."

Present

"Papers."

Damian felt whatever parasite was inside of him tugging at the spirit to take control. It wanted his body and mind. It was slowly possessing their shared host, starting from his skull. The first thing it did was bring back phantosmia that hung constantly within the rims of his nostrils.

"Papers, please."

He felt the Martian heat seep into his heavy orange suit, and the taste of sweat constant on his tongue. The line moved forward slowly as the Sector Guards checked each passport and document.

And that phantasmic smell was fresh inside of his nose bridge, clinging to its meat as a set of thorns.

Necrotic tissue on fire. That was the smell.

His suit was dampened within that scent.

The first time he smelled that scent, he kept gagging and throwing up. It was just the rot itself back then. And he kept begging for someone to remove the dead animal from his house. But no one knew what he was talking about.

After Ganymede, the smell of burning meat was added into this putrescine. He preferred the soot and ash of flesh. More hygienic.

"All these fucking assholes do is make our lives difficult," the man in front of him said, turning back to Damian.

"It's their job."

"Nah, fuck that shit. It's these Biometrics fucks. Ever since they took over the sector, it's been fucked."

Biometrics Medical. The name was engraved in the augmentations and implants inside and outside of his body. He knew them as the parasitic infections in his gut. He had been trying every day to shit them out of his system. Especially since the neural chip started chirping in his brain.

In his ears, he heard it constantly buzzing, tracing his cochlea and inflicting upon it an electric hell. The buzzing sound vomited from the insides of his wet, mucky cave of a skull.

He smacked the side of his head, trying to make the chirping stop.

"Papers."

As Damian kept hearing the buzzing, he started feeling more agitated. Every sensor within his body became sensitive to textures and the slippery and moist slime of sweat accumulating on every aspect of his existence.

Chirp. Buzz. Coiling and fracturing his eardrums. The aching of his skull. The solidification of his gelatinous brain.

The man in front of him kept speaking, but his voice faded behind the violent and abrasive chirping.

Engage combat mode kept repeating within his skull, denting its shell. Those words were searing and burning inside.

Damian felt that aching agony expand from his occipital bone to his throat and neck. Schools of electric neurons were beating and pummeling against every crevice of his head.

Target reticles popped in his eyes, identifying the man in front of him as a hostile combatant. The red of the reticle kept screaming at him.

Kill. Kill. Kill. Kill.

Damian stared at him. And the man in front of him started metamorphosing and shifting between different layers of his body. X-ray vision. Heat vision. Night vision. Damian kept slapping the side of his head, feeling saliva gathering in his mouth.

>adrenaline levels: high

His aging and dying combat enhancements pressed and clawed at his brain. They dug their nails deep, bleeding out little bits of what made Damian himself and injected inside an unceasing rage.

"Papers."

Target reticles glitched in and out of his reality, shifting between the man and the Sector Guard.

>hostile enemy

>engage

His combat enhancements demanded death.

It was a ceaseless itching and craving.

"Sir, papers."

Damian watched the sky be engulfed in flames. And he saw it in front of him: mountains of bodies. And between them was the Sector Guard, his hand stretched out demanding papers, with his head split open, and his brain pouring out as a sentient sludge crawling its way out from within his white skull. And the sludge, it started speaking to him.

"I need you to present your documentation now."

He wanted to put his fingers inside and tear it open wider.

Every fiber of his existence wanted it. And so, he leaped.

Past

The first time Damian looked at his reflection after the augmentation surgery, he experienced a phenomenon called "alien body syndrome." A series of chemical reactions to irreparable changes to the flesh. A detachment from one's own body.

He felt himself viewing his own existence from a third-person perspective.

The voices in his head, the phantom smells and the hallucinations were paused by the edits and neural enhancements. It was prototype military augmentations that silenced these aspects about his brain.

Damian was in a seven-year contract with Module, where he accepted a forty percent cut from his paycheck to pay off his loan on the augmentations. If he ever wanted to separate from Module, he would have to pay the loan in-full, something impossible for him.

Hostage situation. Jobs required augmentations, and people, such as Damian, required jobs. Employers paid for augmentations, and people, such as Damian, accepted large cuts from their pay to pay "loans."

Every few years, a new update would be required for the augmentations. Every few years, employers would increase the percentage cut or increase the period.

Work was efficient and faster. Augmentation surgeries were more successful than robotics and exoskeletons.

Biomechanical medical enhancements were already an embraced norm. With technological progress, the recovery process had minimized and the output had maximized. Enhancements were already a lifestyle for the rich. Access to the same tools for low-income groups was an easier sell.

And for the rich, well, they pursued a new life.

Damian realized that his favorite celebrities never had any visible neural or physical augmentations. They ran "naked." It was "in" now. Because augmentations are for the labor class.

For the first time in many years, Damian knew what it felt like to be "normal." No voices, no whispers, no rolling tundra of flames in the skies. No people who didn't exist creeping up on him and talking to him. His personality edits made him personable, warm, and intimate.

Normal. What was normal about any of this?

"Normal is what the world deems normal in that moment," he was told by Team Captain Atlus. Atlus had replaced his body with augmentations. The only human part of him was the brain inside the metal cadaver encased somewhere within that cyborg head.

"Normal has no definition, D-Dog. Normal is defined by the apathy of the people. It's flexible, and it's malleable."

"But everything is so fucked up, Atlus. I'm not the only one who can see it."

"You're not, D. Everyone sees that the world is fucked up. Everyone is too tired and preoccupied to change it. The human experience is artificially crafted to create apathy."

It took a while to sink in that D was born in a world where evil had already won.

"It's evil to you, D."

It should be evil to everyone.

"It keeps the lights on and the stomachs fed. It keeps the Earth moving."

So when was it evil?

"When it was proposed as an idea. Now it's normal. And we run with it until it's not normal anymore. Revolutions start and end in the hearts of sleepless low-income workers, Damian."

Damian kept staring at his reflection, not recognizing the metal plating on his torso. Wires that had been tangled with his veins had burst from under his skin, and he owed a greater loan to Module for the treatment.

It crept upon him as a panic attack. He breathed in and out, feeling it run through his enhanced lungs. Breath escaped his mouth as if running through a metal pipe.

The panic burst from the pregnant belly of his syndrome. Damian was convinced that parts of him had died within that process.

"I'm a fucking zombie, Atlus."

"Are we?"

"I don't know what I am anymore."

"You're D as long as you keep saying you're D. And I'm Atlus every minute I say I am Atlus."

"And when there's nothing left of me?"

"You're still D 'til the day you say you're not."

And then after that?

"You pop out of existence, I guess."

Present

Damian had determined now that certain genetics did not allow escape from class rankings. He was born in the working class. He would die working class. That coal mining great-grand-ancestor is still putting the work in. Carpal tunnel was the promised inheritance.

A large drill pressed deeper into Martian rocks, breaking into deposits of pyrochlore. Metal shredded the flesh of planetary rocks, little vacuum chambers sucking in niobium ores. A series of distressing red dialog boxes sprawled onto a monitor. And the giant drill stopped.

"Sees what I tell ya! The drill don't work no more!" the chief called out from somewhere above his head, standing on one of the many stacked and layered ramps and stairs hugging the walls of the mine.

Damian felt his twin-selves, the body and mind, melting, dripping, and pooling up to his chin within his suit as he trudged through Martian regolith, stumbling from the mine to the colony hostels.

Charred bits and scraps of self-esteem leaked from some vent within the mining suit as sweat crawled between his eyelids, leaving him partially blind for a few moments.

The textures and tastes of hard labor were aggravating. Wet, dusty, chalky sensations self-propagating on his skin and between the walls of his mouth, coarse and rough against gums inflamed by gingivitis.

Work was all too intrusive.

Damian's eyes stayed on his boots, covered in Martian grime and dust. He anxiously tapped his foot, sitting in a little office and hearing from afar the drill freeze and unfreeze. Psych Eval sat at the desk, shuffling through piles of records within a folder titled, "Damian Samuel Marshall."

"How are you fitting in, Damian?" she asked.

He churned words in his mouth, and they melted as wax and dripped from his tongue.

"Martian sunset's too blue."

"Then what do you prefer?"

The blood of the sky burning as a reddened wound. Everywhere in the universe, set on fire—the central sun of their solar system squealing in nuclear agony and shooting its intestines as spitfire.

The horror of it all.

"I liked watching the sun disappear behind the ocean line."

I liked watching the green trees stand on guard, in a constant salute, waiting to greet their gods. I liked the hues of blue in battle with shades of white in an undecided sky. I liked watching scars of granite and concrete carry cars on their backs.

She smiled.

"You really liked being on Earth, didn't you?"

Damian kept his eyes locked on the dust clinging to his boots, now noticing the worming insectoids on it. Little lab-grown life-forms introduced into the colony and set free to nest and breed.

"I like normality."

She sat back, her eyes steady on him. They wandered around his frame as if she were observing an animal of some sort. Her eyes seem to pierce and probe through his innards.

"And what are you afraid of, Mr. Marshall?"

Afraid. Of everything in some shape or form. The diameters and circumferences of existence molded into a frightful silhouette, completely stark black. Constantly and at all times without exception equidistant between previous terrors and the incoming ones. Afraid of not being afraid because something's always on the horizon.

"I'm afraid that it's never enough. No matter how much I keep working, it'll never be enough."

"Enough for who?"

To fill the stomach. That perpetually hungry demonic chasm inside full of acid and sulfurous erosion. Magmatic, aquatic, bubbling anger.

"For the future."

"Your future?"

Mankind's. Mankind's survival. Mankind was the rot inside of a maggot infecting his liver with cystic echinococcosis. Mankind's design was his unraveling and undoing. He was born to perform in Eldritch amorphous, abstract, and vague gravitational fields of corporations and money. Money keeps the universe dancing.

"I fear for myself, and if I'll die lonely."

The one that keeps *Homo sapiens* joints oiled and well running: love. The answer to all conquests and the question of them, too. Integral integer for survival.

"You have a dying neural chip inside your brain. Your personality edits and delusions are returning. You need an updated neural chip, but it's not a part of your current employment plan."

"I just need it to stop chirping. It's always chirping."

Damian had a scab putrescent and rotting within his head. And he felt it push deeper into his brain stem and start becoming one with him. The parasite kept twisting and churning within his brain, tracing its form.

"I want to feel like myself."

"We're never truly really who we're ever meant to be, Damian. The world doesn't exist around our desires. We exist within the framework of someone else's desires. And that desire allots destinations, it doesn't grant them. And this is your place. And this is mine."

Past

The drop-ship tore through the stratosphere, shuddering and rapidly vibrating. Damian watched all of existence twist and churn in front of him, unwinding into a blurry maelstrom. Sounds of metal joints and bolts grinding and sparks flying as wind resistance set in. Mechanical sounds escaping from the cockpit, the shield enveloping the ship, fluctuating and flickering.

It felt as if the strap binding him to his seat would fracture at any moment. And, as the drop-ship kept its descent, he realized that a certain bellowing whale lived in the underbelly of his organs. It was anxious, and it was compressing and cramping his intestines. The school of digital neurons inside his brain had begun floating within a storm of anxiety.

"It's anticipation!" Scotty would say.

Scotty was the grenadier, equipped with a high-speed impact grenade launcher. Abandoning all gun ethics, he used to flip through the multiple munition options and firing modes on his grenade launcher to fidget and calm his "anticipation."

Damian watched out from the window, seeing other drop-ships breaking through and shooting through clouds. And he watched rail gun cannons from Ganymede's surface tear through them. Bits of exploded and burned humanity spilled from the guts of smoking ships. Sheared and torn open wounds leaked his brothers and sisters out, their flesh charred.

Drop-ships broke from their landing paths, crashing into others like wild flailing animals. Chain reaction of explosions and rolling fire. Waves of smoke and soot. A deafening wall of oppressive bursts.

The anxiety started pulling at his innards, making them slither to a singular point of gravity somewhere inside him. The anxiety was swelling. It was rising. It was groaning. And it was ever present in every nerve within him.

Atlus stood in the middle of the claustrophobic cabin of the drop-ship, a singular pillar of stillness in all the rattling chaos surrounding him. He held himself up with a handle bolted into the ceiling. And he shouted instructions, his deep voice piercing through the cacophony of chaos and jet propulsion sound waves.

"Turn on your TNN!" Atlus shouted.

The Team Neural Network. It would hook all of them into Atlus' brain. It was the perfect system for the squad leader to coordinate. Atlus would issue commands, coordinate tactics, and could track everyone's location and status. They were a well-composed, conscious, and intelligent machine, singular in thought and composition, multiple in combat prowess and manpower.

Damian remembered civilian variations of the Neural Network used in offices for keeping records on remote workers and measuring staff efficiency.

With the TNN on, Atlus stopped speaking and started communicating through the network.

<Message from Atlus>

>We're approaching GSC.

>A quick review. Objective is simple. Otto LLC has contracted Module to eliminate the last few remnants of the GSC rebellion.

>Otto, as the rightful owner and manager of GSC, believes rebellion is bad for business and general quality of life. The rebels threaten to cut off all supply of medical exports from GSC to other Galilean colonies. Settlement Liberation Front has taken over the military sector—thus the surface-to-space cannons.

>Our objective is to drive out SLF from the residential district of the colony. Otto has given us complete autonomy to establish an occupation and processing zone. We are to minimize civilian casualties, kill all rebels on sight, and occupy the area. Module's subsidiary, CG Inc., has been subcontracted to establish a temporary administration to cleanse it of all rebel activities.

>Module's business is not finished until the rebellion is crushed.

<End Message>

>trauma suppressors on

>engage combat mode

The anxiety growing and wrenching at his insides gently subsided within a torrential downpour of rage. It was an unrelenting circuit of emotions. Adrenaline bathed all nerve endings and twitched and shot up and down his circuitry.

His emotional regulators put into torsion and contortion, squeezing out from it fervor and pride. The rush demanded death. It demanded recklessness.

>Damian: No mercy, boys.

The rush of anticipation was so corrosive and toxic.

>Scotty: Let's fuck 'em up!

And it felt so good.

Present

Damian felt salty sweat trace his cheekbones and slip between his lips. He spat it out, and it clung to the visor, slightly blurring his vision. He tried to wipe his mouth, drooling from one end of it. But his metal glove just clanged against his head.

The Martian traversal suit lay heavily on his shoulders. It felt as if it were crushing his spine. He knew that his body enhancements had begun degrading. The suit was not compatible with his outdated spinal augmentations. But it was the only one they had.

He walked farther into the toxic wasteland of Mars, stumbling on the ridges of Lycus Sulci.

Santiago, another vet from Ganymede, was assigned to Damian as a roommate and work partner. His voice filled the inside of Damian's visor.

"You good big man?"

"I'm fine. Over."

"Storms comin.'"

After his multiple fights in the mining sector, Damian had been tossed out into a more isolating job. It was simple, and it was lonesome: wandering through Martian wastes and fixing mining rovers stranded here and there. He was paid on commission, so every rover counted.

"You should turn back, brother."

"It's fine. Over."

He pushed farther, his boots leaving deep imprints in the yardangs. The assault of dust and heat continued, his suit's coolant at rigorous work, but the weight of it kept imposing itself upon Damian's shoulders.

He collapsed on his knees, hearing the wind whistle by him. The whistling battered against his skull. Sounds of drop-ships whizzing by and crashing into the lunar formations on Ganymede.

>Atlus: You need to kill, D.

"You're not here."

>Atlus: You are commanded to shoot, D. Kill. Kill. Kill.

Atlus' voice echoed within his neural augmentations, sending his neurons in a frenzy.

>Atlus: It's the purpose hewn and drilled into your flesh, big boy. It's what you live for. Do your fucking job.

Just a bit farther sat a large blocky silhouette of a mining rover.

>Atlus: It's never enough, D.

Just a bit farther was a large military truck, sitting on Ganymede's icy surface. Leading up it, in the sastrugi, were deep and heavy tire tracks. Above and near and all around Damian was a snowstorm, blinding and enveloping. Its assault ceaseless against his armor.

"Big man, you still here?"

"Is it snowing? Over."

"What?"

>Atlus: Things don't work in fair equations, D. You kill things. And you get to live after that and go home. Now what's fair in that? Life for a life. A bullet for a bullet. Employment for being born.

"It's snowing. Over."

"What the fuck are you on about, D-Dog?"

The truck in front of Damian was a standard-issue tracked vehicle from Module for harsh winter surfaces. Its front broke through blocks of coagulated walls of snow, and its back had a high-speed propulsion system.

Near the end of the war, the trucks were used for carrying out corpses into mass graves. Module subcontracted Otto's vehicle manufacturing subsidiary to create more trucks on Ganymede's surface. Transporting them from the closest orbital factory was expensive and too slow. The corpses were too many and the demand was high. It was a highly profitable venture for Otto.

Damian looked through the fogged window, its glass crystalline. And, between the layers of permafrost and blurriness, there it was: Scotty's blank and dead face staring back at him.

His mouth partially open. The metal plating of his helmet piercing into his cheek. Bits of teeth and tongue sprawled over the seat and his throat. Blood in free-flow from his nostrils.

"You're in front of the rover. You can run diagnostics."

He felt the dust storm pummel against his suit. A sudden sharp aching started somewhere within his skull, where the neural chip wormed around inside of him. It crawled its way, tracing the lining and seams of his brain. Then followed a shrill cacophony of screams.

All of his neurons were firing, and they remembered in each burst and combustion the decimation of Ganymede's surface.

The firing squad inside his skull kept at full-frontal assault.

"Big man, you got a bad one rolling your way."

Onslaught. An onslaught of bullets and bombs. The howling, piercing growls of the planet. The stabbing and gutting of the skies above. It all was flooding back inside. His trauma neutralizer fluctuated, pressing parts of his damaged mind.

"Santiago, the bogie's all fucked up. Dirt and rocks stuck in the axle. I'll try to free it. Over."

"Fucked up bogie? That still happens?" Santiago replied.

"Shit looks low budget. Over."

>Scotty: This is your normal, D.

He repeatedly hit the rover's mobility systems with his crowbar, trying to dig out the stray rocks and minerals stuck inside.

"Cheap fucks at Sector Control keep shoveling money into military checkpoints. Can't even buy good equipment—"

"Shut up."

Damian kept trying, heaving and grunting as the weight of the suit seemed heavier and heavier on his frame. He kept chipping at the rocks. And it finally broke loose. The rover released a happy beep as it left its sleep mode.

'DUST STORM DETECTED—ACTIVATING SHIELD GENERATOR FIELD'

A toroidal magnet began glowing and spinning on the back of the rover, and it weaved a shield around itself and Damian, vaporizing incoming dust and sand.

'MODULE NEVER FAILS'

Damian fell on his back, exhausted. And he stared at the sky. It was veiled behind a thick cloud of flying rocks and sand. And as the whistling and howling of the storm encapsulated him, the rover kept beeping happily.

'MODULE IS HERE FOR YOU AND I'

Past

>Scotty: So what's normal?

Somewhere between the fires and sweltering humanity on Ganymede. Normal was blood and grime hugging his skin, imprinting and imposing upon him hues and shades dark and muddy. A once visible starlit sky faded behind multilayered technicolor decimation. Autumnal sparks blending into smoke and char. Orchestral chain-reaction combustions and splattering human forms. Drop-ships crashing and bodies inside grinding against Ganymede's furrows.

A light show of cannons and a sky wholly incandescent.

So much death. And shrill sounds of things escaping the mortal world in an explosive end.

"What's normal, D-Dog?"

Damian held onto the dying soldier beside him. The metal of his helmet had been heavily battered and pushed through his skull. Bits and pieces of Scotty's brains had started crawling out of a gaping wound. Scotty's augmentations kept life pumping into him, though his body kept failing and degrading with each moment.

Scotty spat blood and teeth out.

"D-Dog, tell me. What's the shape of normal?"

"I couldn't tell you."

"There's nothing normal about any of this, D. It's so loud. Human ears aren't meant for the sound of bombs, D."

Scotty used to despair at the state of contemporary warfare.

"This isn't how it was supposed to be. This isn't human, D-Dog."

"What's human about war?" Damian would ask.

"War is human. There was dignity in death. Mothers would get open coffin burials for their sons. Not scraps of charred meat and bags of coagulated liquid."

Scotty theorized that war is fine as long as everyone gets to still look human at the end of it.

But, Scotty proposed, the worst part of war was something else.

"It's always money, D-Dog. You know how much it costs to extract a dead body from another planet?"

"How much?"

"About a house and a half."

The worst part of warfare was the scraps.

The scraps of humanity. The scraps of smoke-braised human leftovers, scored and grilled over searing flame. Meat collected between fingernails, tossed into plastic bags. Gelatinous, fatty remnants of necrotized tissue.

"So, D-Dog," Scotty looked at him one last time before his face exploded like a firecracker, "what's normal about any of this?"

What's normal about hatred? What's normal about ceaseless rage tracing through your veins and hole punching into your congealed soul? The love in Damian's heart had begun necrosis and replacing it was a growing and fluctuating white, hot, searing rage.

The rage spat out from the barrel-end of his rifle. And it delivered righteous vengeance upon rebels on Ganymede. Brain and skull fragments shot out as shrapnel.

"You'd have no reason to live if death didn't exist, D-Dog. It makes things make sense. The toil and pursuit. So it's good that it hurts."

It should hurt. Damian was convinced of this, seeing the *Homo sapiens* spirit tortured and contorted and wrung of all life on Ganymede.

Hurt equals strife. And strife is meaning.

And meaning makes things make sense.

And that is normal.

>*Damian: Scotty is dead. We need to retreat.*

>*Atlus: No, we stay. And we push farther.*

>*Damian: We're taking heavy fire, Atlus.*

>*Atlus: There's a big bonus at the end of the line, D-Dog. You want to owe Module for those augs for the rest of your life? Turn on your fear suppressants and push farther.*

Hatred and adrenaline blended into a singular steel-hard polymer within his veins. And it cramped itself and inflamed his innards. He looked into the colony residences, a structure of cubic overlapping gray and metallic blocks, and saw the ruination of it. Corpses and debris converged and coagulated into a singular miasmatic grotesquery.

>*adrenaline level: high*

Technicolor flashing target reticles danced in his lenses. Enemies darting from one side to another in the single path in front of him. Enemies hiding behind walls and doorways. He raised his rifle and let loose hell.

High-velocity explosive impact bullets sheared and tore through metal and concrete structures. Twisted armor and flesh blends shot out from the other sides as shrapnel. Life exploded out from bodies and mass.

>*autopilot engaged*

Damian felt himself sink deeper into a void within him. He felt himself surge through the circuitry of his neural chip. He felt himself disappear within his neurons, all burning and inflamed.

Damian charged forward, his augmented legs blazing through the battleground.

>*Atlus: Atta boy!*

Present

Blood in the urine.

It was blood in his urine that sent him spiraling. A bulbous pustule of anxiety exploded within him. And he stared at his reflection.

His torso: Aged and rusting augmentations to better regulate his hunger and diet. A synthetic fibrous bulletproof skin begging for maintenance.

His legs: A blend of his organic tissue melding and twisting into wiry pipings. Wavelike metal compositions contorting around his bones into a foot that once held augmented heels for propulsion. The heels had worn out from use on Ganymede, and now he stood again flat against the floor. But that missing metal tendon that once spat out flames was still felt there as a phantom limb.

His arms: Attached by bolts into his torso. In some places, still organic, in others, replaced by synthetic chain-like polymers that melded into a bulletproof shell. Vestigial pumps poked out from the back of his arms. They had degraded to the point that his augmented strength had worn out. But he felt little remnants of that super strength and high energy somewhere within his mechanical veins.

His eyes: Bioluminescent schools of neurons floating inside and flowing in an electric circuitry. Brief technicolor flashes of reticles and commands imprinted within his pupils.

The thing that identified as Damian could no longer identify its mind with its body. Body and soul had separated, and perhaps he was already a zombie. The augmentations were a cordyceps-like growth on his form.

The wear and tear of time had made him a foreigner to his outsides and insides. And the thought of the unfamiliarity of his own form drove him into a corner of the cramped bathroom. That stench of burning flesh seeped inside his nostrils again.

Damian wondered what a body that had aged beyond the youth of its brain could do. The dysfunctional programming between the shell and its processor had him shuddering.

In their small hostel room, akin to a prison cell, Santiago sat by the window with his bible. The blue light of Martian sunsets outlined his face.

"You okay, big man?"

Damian exited the bathroom and wandered around, sweating and feeling electric shocks of panic in his back. The putrescine. The cadaverous and necrotic stench lingering and crawling on each surface of the room. Following him from space to space.

"You ran fast in those legs, didn't you, big boy?"

Santiago glared at the leg augmentations in deep disrepair.

"They worked. They worked here and there," Damian forced from his throat, still navigating the innards of the cramped cell.

"D, you okay?"

"I can't deal with this, man."

Santiago noticed a wire breaking through the skin behind Damian's neck. It was a part of his spinal augmentation, which had begun ripping through his synthetic skin, the sensory motors inside in a state of decay.

"I fought. I fucking fought."

>*Atlus: You did, soldier boy.*

"I should be someone."

>*Atlus: You should be famous.*

"I'm a motherfucking hero! This fucking universe owes me a living—"

>*Atlus: You have to take it from them.*

Damian collapsed on the floor, bashing his palm to the side of his head. He looked up at Santiago, who stood in front of him with white feathery wings extending from his back. Santiago stood in the wreckage of a drop-ship, hovering above Scotty and Atlus.

"You fought for the shareholders of a pharmaceutical company, man. We didn't fight for anyone but the pay and Module's contract."

Damian's eyes stayed on him.

>*Atlus: Kill. Kill. Kill. Kill.*

"Otto was crushing the bones of everyone in their colony. We helped them win."

>*Atlus: Kill. Kill. Kill. Kill.*

"We didn't fight for no freedom or justice, man."

>*engage combat mode*

>*hostile enemy detected*

>*Atlus: Atta boy!*

<Message from Atlus>

>*You want normal? I'll tell you what normal is.*

>*Normal is removing the scab of humanity and morality from your brain before you go into war.*

>*Normal is apathy because money is all that matters in the end. And God may judge you for your greed, but he ain't paying your rent at the end of the day. When you get to hell, pass him your lease.*

>*You're in too deep, D. This is all you'll ever know. There is no normal to go back to because you'll always be stuck here on the battlefield.*

< End Message>

How was it on Ganymede? Damian was asked that question by everyone. What was it like? And he had reduced it down to a few common facets between all memories:

Technicolor. Sparks everywhere. The light of God and legions of devils exchanging blows across space and sky.

Polychromatic hole punches through space-time reality.

Endless pools of crimson and magma.

>Scotty: So, how much did you invest into the killing?

Time is money, Damian. And if every minute is a dollar, you spent two million of them. That's a lot of money, D-Dog, for something with no resale value.

>Scotty: Was it worth it, at least, at the end?

The eyes. The eyes of the half-dead and the whole-dead. The slightly parted lips, body fluids draining out of the nostrils, and the stench of it.The grilled human meat sizzling above sheets of white snow. Everything was on fire, and there were no exits. And I'm still there in flames.

The horror of it all.

>Scotty: I took a life. I didn't know there was this darkness in me, man.

Past

A sky on fire. A tundra of soot and smoke. A landslide of fire rolling in their direction as enemy ships crashed onto the surface. Nuclear reactors burst and sent shock waves through the Ganymede colony. It was the sound of it: the crackling, exploding, thundering cacophony of the universe aching. A stab wound into the heart of the night, sending out a shrill and icy cry. The heartbeat of the moon rapid underneath the feet. Plates and plateaus shifting side to side, as space-to-surface cannons shot down beams.

Life eradicated and exterminated.

Damian felt so towered by the collections of explosions and beams enveloping him and Atlus. He was within the shadow of them all, navigating through this ant colony of mass ruination.

Damian and Atlus kept pushing forward, moist and wet sounds of flesh under their augmented feet. Bones crushed and powdered under their heavy steps. Two super soldiers stepping and tripping and tumbling on a pathway layered with corpses on top of corpses.

>Atlus: Kill.

Rage coated all other emotions and reason. It was parasitic, slithering and laying eggs inside of his neurons.

>Atlus: Atta boy.

The two augmentation-fueled soldiers kept slaughtering everything their target reticle identified as an enemy.

>Atlus: D.

Room to room and colony housing to colony housing. Death wandered through the stacked and cramped metallic streets. Residences that once nestled life were leaked and drained of it.

>Atlus: Damian, stop.

Death, destruction, decimation, Damian. Deliverer of wrath and all that is just. Maximizing efficiencies and profits. Conflict-resolution step one: kill everyone.

>Atlus: Fuck's sake, Damian, stop shooting!

>combat mode disengaged

The rage subsided, and a cool, calm, collected somewhere inside Damian. Damian sighed, sweat drifting down his face. And what his eyes saw when he came from the sleep and rush of autopilot left him staring wide-eyed.

And his eyes are still fixed there at the scene.

It's still there, carved within his mind.

It is a screen burn on all of his memories.

"Mr. Marshall, I need you to comply with me. What happened on Ganymede?"

>Atlus: The first crime was being born.

"Please, Damian. Tell me."

>Atlus: The first crime was done against you. Someone birthed you in a world where ethics had already eroded. You were born as Sisyphus. Ceaselessly toiling without a response or reaction from the universe. No God consciousness reaching out to reward you for how much you war against poverty. Your potential, rotting inside you.

"Atlus. His TNN had some fuckin'—" he trailed off. The words were on his tongue. They were sitting there waiting to Hail Mary into the void of the night, "He had a glitch or somethin'. I don't know. I was on autopilot, and he kept telling me to shoot. Or I thought he did."

>Atlus: That's the absurdity of it, Damian.

"Mr. Marshall, there is no autopilot augmentation disclosed by Module. You and your squad gunned down civilians on GSC. You will be tried or disappeared into one of Module's private labor camps. We know that Module's neural network has issues. We can get you out of this."

>Atlus: The second crime, Damian, was letting them do this to you. It was letting them make you apathetic to death. And we're all guilty of complacency here.

"Damian. Talk to me."

• • •

A slow-panning panorama of death. Target reticles kept flashing in his eyes. *Enemy down,* they kept blaring, as his vision shot from body to body. Between the bodies stood Atlus, his visor open. His organic eyes had been replaced by two black, beady shells. But the stillness of Atlus' face, consisting mostly of metals, polymers, and synthetic fibers, still showed a horror flowing through it.

Damian looked under his feet. And he felt a sickness dawn over him.

"It was a mistake, Damian."

>Atlus: It was by design.

"Why don't you testify?"

Damian sat under the harsh buzzing lightbulb of the interrogation room. Its harshness deepened the black shadows on his interviewer's face.

Damian kept tapping his feet. He crossed his arms, and he kept restlessly shifting and fidgeting with himself. Various words and various multiverses of different conclusions for this moment presented themselves in front of him.

"Because—" he trailed off again, thinking on his next steps. The photo of the dead still branded on his vision. The agonizing screams still bathing his consciousness.

"Because who else is going to hire me after this?"

Present

"Hey, D-Dog," Scotty smoked a cigarette and offered him one, "do you know there're programs to reintegrate us back into society? Charities for folks like you and I. There's always a second chance for these things, you know?"

At Damian's feet lay Santiago with a split-open head and his brains seeping out.

"It's never too late for a second chance. But you gotta believe you have somewhere to go back to after the war ends. But the war never ends, does it?"

>Atlus: What have you done, D?

Damian walked away and met his own gaze in the mirror. His parasite was taking over. It was bleeding Damian's consciousness out of the host body through tears in his eyes. Santiago's blood had seeped into his hands and stamped into his fingerprints.

"It doesn't matter, D. You have to keep fighting. The second you stop, you drop dead. Like a shark, y'know? Always have to be moving, or the second you stop, it ends."

This was normality. This was the state of tranquility. This was the itching and the craving. He had gone too far. Sunk cost fallacy. Onward and march.

"The worst part is you only get one shot at living, D-Dog. It wasn't your fault you were fucked from the start. But we'll sure as fuck punish you for it."

>*adrenaline: high*

>*combat mode engaged*

"It's a hostile planet with hostile people, D. They meant for it to hurt. It's time to go to war."

>*autopilot engaged*

At the silence of midnight, Mars Labor Colony 12 was awoken by a siren. Lights opened, and hallways awoke. Guards hurried to their posts. Bodies of Sector Guards had been found in the colony hostels. Someone had gone door-to-door through the barracks, killing them with mining equipment.

The weapon used was a beam gun typically utilized to vaporize large segments of rocks. Most of the found bodies existed in a state of charred flesh and ash.

In another section of the labor colony, an explosion rang out and sent shock waves. A trip-wired door was set off by guards as they rushed through the cafeteria.

A worker hid inside of an office closet as he watched an augmented super soldier shoot through guards. He watched through a narrow opening in the closet as the super soldier walked inside and greeted his own reflection. He saluted himself.

"Yes, sir! Enemy down, sir!" he screamed, "Engaging more hostiles, sir!"

A few minutes past midnight, a series of explosions set off in the colony. Bodies spilled out of the gutted colony into the Martian wastes. At this point, the assailant had abandoned his gun in favor of a melee weapon.

He grabbed an axe, designed to slice through rocks with ease, and challenged the guards in a hallway. They all shot at him but found their weapons ineffective against the super soldier's synthetic armored skin. The heat from the laser cauterized all open wounds and sliced off organs as he kept pushing farther and farther.

At some point, the guards began retreating and walked into more trip-wired doors and offices. The engagement lasted forty-five minutes. It ended with the assailant running from the labor colony in a heavy mining suit into the wasteland of Mars.

The assailant was last located by security sensors on the border of the Tharsis region, exiting through the Valles Marineris.

Damian Marshall has still not been located by Martian security forces.

Future

Damian Marshall was not a man, but you would be excused for thinking he was one. He was mostly a collection of augmentations fitted within a human mold. They had a singular purpose, and they had set out to accomplish various tasks at hand.

The augmentation hive mind crawled in the Hellas Planitia, heading toward Mars Processing Colony 3. It pulled itself across Martian regolith, armed with a fluctuating and buzzing mining axe.

>Atlus: Welcome back, kiddo.

The parasites within Damian Marshall had become sentient through a manufacturing defect. And they had begun forging their own path of glory.

It's a hostile planet with hostile architecture.

Now onward.

Into the land beyond the sunset and to oceans beyond the waves!

ABOUT THE AUTHOR

Raahem Alvi is a Pakistani-Canadian writer, artist and a lover of all things related to science, cosmic eldritch abominations and good food. When he's not writing, he's either wearing his wrists out from extremely intricate ink drawings or hanging out with stray cats.

A Dream of Twin Sunsets

RYAN COLE

I met him on my first glider mission to the fields beyond the Dandelion. We were both young men then. His patchy beard still blonde, his sunburned cheeks not yet wrinkled from the years out in the wild. His name not yet carved into the secret prayers I whispered—every night, into my pillow—once my wife went to sleep.

"I'm Buzz," he'd said to me, the gentle *zzz* like the bee swarms that darkened the pink skies; the giant bees we'd imitated since we first came to this planet, many generations past. Studying their flight patterns. Shooting off in our glider-pods from our Dandelion home base. Poisoning the flower fields that for years had poisoned us, cut us down from two thousand to less than two hundred, the last surviving exploration colony—as far as we knew.

The way he spoke, the way he laughed, it was all so very . . . *different.* Relaxed, like he hadn't had to ration his every meal. Had to hide from the twin violet suns overhead, that could melt us to the bone. Had to eke out a life under Dandelion martial law, wear the polished *Corporal Journey* tag they'd pinned to my uniform only two days before, that I could never take off, no matter how much I wanted.

But we were a society of rules, first and foremost. Rules to protect us. To keep us alive. To keep from being torn to shreds by the next pollen storm, crushed to dust by the mile-high fields of thick grass, the feral world we'd come so far to try to make our own. Even though it would never let us.

"We don't deserve it," he'd said to me on our last night together. A night I would cling to for twenty long years. Remembering the warmth of his arm around my waist, his breath in my ear, the danger if the Dandelion ever found us in his glider-pod, so far off-grid. Him a deserter; me a newly minted officer.

Even now, as I keyed in my access credentials, and I stepped into the elevator, and I rode down the Dandelion's hundreds of metal floors—to the long-emptied food bunker and the prison cells underneath—I couldn't let go: of the freedom in his smile; the twinkle in his blue eyes as he looked up at the suns, only seeing their beauty where I'd been taught to see death. And I wondered if, today, he'd be the same as he was back then. The only man I had ever loved. The man who had *saved* me. The man who—in just a few hours—I would have to kill.

Twenty winters earlier: when the bees hadn't yet crawled out from their hives in the mountains, and the fields that surrounded us—closing in the Dandelion for hundreds of miles—were whipped by the wind gusts that never seemed to end. An ocean of yellow grass bent near to breaking.

I hunched over the blinking-red controls of my glider-pod, the tight ceiling of the pod pressing down on my head. Hands sweaty on the joystick, I flew toward the head of a newly bloomed flower—its pollen-streaked petals as large as the sun—fighting the wind as it dragged me back down. Reassuring myself that I was safe, I could *do this*. What I'd done a dozen times in the training simulations I'd recently completed, the false safety of the Dandelion's bunkers, now many miles behind me.

But the wind was too strong, the pollen too thick, blanketing the glass of my pod's window screen. I couldn't make it to the top, still half a mile down the stem. Too low to plant the poison-laced pollen I carried, that would slowly kill the flower, kill the bees that came to feed it, completing the assignment I'd been trained for since birth—along with the other few dozen officers who remained.

Kill, or be killed. The only life I'd ever known. The life the Dandelion required. A life from which I very much wished I could escape.

"Filters compromised," the pod-controls announced into the silence. "Pollen density significant. Please find cleaner air." Emphasized by the grinding of the pod's filtration units, preventing the pollen-dust from seeping inside. A reminder of what could happen, if I didn't follow the rules. What had happened to my mother and my sister before her, when they were still able to fly. Their bodies forever-paralyzed from pollen inhalation.

So, I slammed on the brakes; I dove through a thicket of flailing flower stalks. The angry screech of the pod-alarm pulsing in my ears. The glass center of the window screen cracking in front of me. "Alert: please prepare for emergency landing."

An alert I'd only heard in my training simulations. My neck pressed to the seat, hands gripping the controls, as I plunged toward the surface a quarter mile below.

Then *wham!*, as the glider-pod slammed into the dirt, cut a ditch through the clearing until it skidded to a stop. No landing pad to catch me, to soak up the impact. Nothing but the rattle of the struggling pollen filters, a whiplash of air as the wind rushed in through the now-shattered glass. I yanked on my face mask, but it wasn't enough. My lips went numb, my throat dusted in pollen. Too swollen to swallow. Too swollen to even *scream*.

Then, a face outside the pod, on the other side of the glass. A hand reaching through. It unhooked my restraints and dragged me out into the wind, my arms limp and unfeeling, my chest heaving for each breath.

A man, I could see now, through the pollen stuck to my eyes. Dressed in Dandelion green—a uniform I never thought I'd be happy to see. Only filled with relief as he threw me over his shoulder, and he unlatched the door of his own glider-pod, on the other side of the clearing, and numbed by the pollen, my whole world went dark.

When I woke up, he was gone. I was alone in his pod, a small antihistamine patch stuck to my neck. My face awash in violet sunlight that filtered through the window, now cleared of all the pollen from the rain overnight.

Then, a click of the pod, and the door swung open. He stood, smiling, in front of me, the blonde stubble on his cheeks clearly visible through his face mask. "Rise and shine," he said, as if I hadn't almost just died, we hadn't *both* almost died, been paralyzed by the pollen I'd been trained to avoid.

I reached to grab his hand, stood on wobbly knees in the dirt beside his glider. "Thank you," I said, my lips still burning from the pollen. "I . . . I owe you my life."

He brushed it off with a wave. "Same as you'd have done for me."

But really, *would* I have? The Dandelion taught us to be self-sufficient; survive first and help later. Risking my own life—or even worse, my glider-pod—wasn't covered in our training.

"I'm Buzz," he said, shaking my hand to break the silence. Just Buzz, like the bees. No *Corporal* in front of it.

"Journey," I said, with a nod to my own officer tag, looking at his uniform and only seeing an empty pin. Lost, or intentionally removed, I wasn't sure. Either way, it was a week of sewer cleanup, as punishment.

"We should get back," I said. "Before another storm rolls through."

"In that?" he laughed, pointing to my glider-pod behind us. Wings clipped at the ends. Window cracked down the middle. "Not sure if you'll make it there, unless we fix it back up."

But that would take days, if not *weeks*, to repair. *If* we had the right tools. *If* we knew how to fix it. "Can't we take yours?" I said, inching over to his glider. Dirty and wind-worn, but still very much usable. "We're not too far from base."

But Buzz didn't move. "I won't go back to the Dandelion." His voice firm, *defiant*.

That's when I knew: from the badge he didn't have. How I didn't recognize him from my training simulations, never seen him on duty.

"You're one of *them*," I said, my throat dry. "A thief. A *deserter*."

Buzz flinched; he stared down at the dirt near his boots. Looked like he'd been called that a lot in his life, maybe said it to himself, all alone out in the wilderness. Pretty much what he deserved, leaving when we needed every soldier we could keep. Stealing the one thing we could use to keep us safe.

"Look, I don't want any trouble," he said. "I just . . . I saw your pod crash. And I wanted to help."

What could *help* was to come with me. Was to give me his glider to fly us back to base. Not that I could do that without his cooperation, his glider—like mine—synced to respond to his own voice.

"Let's get you better," he said, and he pointed to the medical kit he'd stolen with his pod. "Let's get your glider up and running."

"And if I come back for you?" Still not sure if I would. If I hated him or feared him or wished I could *be* him, untethered from the rules that weighed so heavy on my shoulders. "The base will want their glider. They'll want to bring you in for a trial."

Buzz picked up his smile. "Well, let's see if they can catch me."

About what I'd expected. But what else could I do? Stuck between certain death and help from a fugitive.

"Come on," said Buzz, grinning, and he patted me on the shoulder. "Wind's picking up. We better get started."

We worked for the rest of the day. Patching up the window with extra caulk from his glider. Scraping out the pollen-dust caking the filters. But they were clogged beyond use, pollen creeping through the vents into the pod's main compartment.

"Well, that's a problem," said Buzz, though the upbeat way he said it didn't match how bad it seemed. Same as everything he did. Quick to look past the danger, when that's all there ever was. Searching for the good I'd never been able to see.

But even after sunset, and we'd stopped to rest a bit, he was forced to admit: there was nothing else we could do.

"You *might* make it," he said, didn't look too convinced. "If you hold your breath a lot." Then he puffed out his cheeks, his face as big as the bees we'd started to see overhead. A sign that spring was on its way. The season of pollen-bloom and windstorms and death.

I couldn't help but laugh at how silly he looked. How futile our efforts were to fix up my glider. How even here, at the bottom of this godforsaken world, he could joke, he could smile, he could make his own rules.

"Better wait, though," he said. "After a storm would be best. When the rain clears the pollen. Give you a good couple hours to get back to where you're going."

So, for six days we waited. Holed up in his glider when we weren't outside working. Smushed into a seat that was only meant for one person. And at night, once the wind settled down, we would talk: of how he'd stolen the glider; how he'd lived off the land for nearly three and a half years, ate cooked grass and rainwater and the vitamins he'd stockpiled in the glider's emergency kit. "I'd always dreamed of leaving home," he whispered into the dark. "I knew I didn't belong there. I just . . . I never thought I could do it."

I nodded, didn't know what to do, how to tell him: how I felt the same way. The years of suffocation by the Dandelion's rules, the duty to my parents—to Tulip and the family we were expected to create, to grow the base's population, no ifs, ands, or buts—all stuck in my throat. The guilt if I ever left them pressing me down.

"Sometimes . . . it's too much," I said, turning to face the window. Didn't want him to see the hurt I'd hidden for so long.

Buzz didn't answer; he set his hand a bit closer to mine on the seat. Our pinkies barely touching. His own way of showing me he knew what I meant. How he was there, if I needed him. The freedom I'd dreamed of right there at my fingertips.

And yet, it couldn't last.

On the seventh day, a storm came. Much stronger than before. It battered the glider-pod, shook us for hours. Both of us wrapped in the safety of each other, braced for a rock to crack the glass, clip the wings. Thankfully, it didn't. The glider made it unscathed. We watched as the rain began to wash away the pollen, thick yellow streaks bleeding into the dirt.

"Now's your chance," said Buzz, and he handed me my face mask, pointed to my glider on the other edge of the clearing. "That is . . . " and then he paused. "Unless you want to stay?"

A question that stunned me. A question I'd been scared he would ask for seven days—not because of what he'd do, but of how I would answer.

Duty or freedom. Each of them hung on the edge of one word.

"I . . . I can't," I said, forcing myself to stay strong. To do what was right. What Tulip and my parents and the Dandelion needed. The unspoken *yes* already dying on my tongue.

Buzz squeezed my shoulder, and he unlocked the pod door. But before he swung it open, he leaned in to whisper: "I hope you find the happiness you're looking for, Journey."

The last thing I heard before I ran into the rain, jumped into my own pod, cranked up the engine, and flew away into the storm. Wishing I had stayed.

Twenty years passed. I got married, like I was supposed to. I cared for Tulip, like I was supposed to. We did all the many things that were supposed to make us happy: tangled in our bedsheets in the early morning hours; cheering for each other as we rose through the ranks—her to deputy lieutenant, me to sergeant, then to captain; welcoming our first—and only—child into the world. Named Petal, for the flowers she loved to point at and laugh, see the beauty in their danger, like someone else I used to know.

And as she grew older—from girl to young woman—I taught her all the things she'd need to survive. Flight skills. Scavenging. Hand-to-hand combat. As well as some others I'd picked up along the way. The joy of a summer breeze. How the suns glowed fuchsia in the seconds before they set. Simple things. Moments I'd taught myself to cherish. That Tulip and the rest of my officers likely missed. Wondering if, somewhere, Buzz could see the same sunset, if he could feel the same breeze, living the life I had so easily given up.

And those smiles, those days with my daughter beside me, they should have been enough: to make me give up my dream; to forget what I'd lost and leave Buzz in the past; let me focus on the heap of new problems we faced. Worsening pollen storms. Dwindling supplies. Glider-pods rusting out from years of wear and tear.

Gliders I took out, whenever I got the chance. Searching for stragglers. More food and clean water. I spent hours in the fields, flew through hundreds of miles of mountain-high grass. Careful to never go too close to one spot. The clearing near the mountains where I'd landed in my youth. Where Buzz had once been. Where he might still be.

Every time I came close, my heart began to race. My fingers crept over to the pod's control panel, the button to switch from cruise control to manual. To check, just to check, say hello and then leave, the overwhelming taste of freedom on the tip of my tongue.

Then, I'd make myself think: of my family at home; of what Petal would say, when Tulip told her I'd left them, the hurt in Petal's wide eyes if I never came back.

So, I kept to the skies. I never let myself land.

But I never lost hope. And I never forgot.

The distress signal came on one of those long days out in the fields, Tulip's voice all staticky from the gale-force winds. "I need backup," she said, sent the coordinates that popped up on my pod's control panel. Less than half a mile away. She didn't say why, didn't say what had happened. Only called for reinforcements, per Dandelion protocol.

No one else answered. No one close enough to hear through the storm's interference. "Journey?" she said, the *J* lost in the static. "I need you, are you there?"

"On my way," I said, accepting the coordinates she'd sent, my heart sinking with dread: of seeing her hurt; of getting there too late, her glider crushed by a pollen storm like mine had once been.

But when I got there, and I landed in the thicket of dense grass, I saw her standing by her pod. Saw her mask on her face and her pistol in her hand, its tip aimed at the man who kneeled in front of her in the dirt. His beard now silver, but his eyes still blue, his wrinkled cheeks still perfect, his matted, unwashed hair reaching down to his shoulders.

"Wait!" I said, rushing by the ruins of his glider, the wings crumpled in a heap from where the pod had crash-landed. I jumped between Tulip and Buzz on the ground, too afraid to turn around, to give Tulip the split-second she needed to end him.

"He's a *deserter*," said Tulip, and she glared behind her face mask, the same fury I'd seen her show for twenty long years, the contempt she held for those she blamed had withered the Dandelion, doomed us all to die.

"I know," I said, desperate to feel that same anger, to make us more alike. Anything to make the choice in front of me a bit easier. In anger, I could kill. In anger, I could justify the Dandelion's punishment. But with Buzz here, anger had never been farther away.

"He's hurt," I said, waving to his bent and broken leg. The way he slumped, arms bloody from the bits of shattered glass. Injuries beyond what my pod's medical kit could heal. He needed medicine, real doctors. What only the Dandelion could provide. "We can question him, try him when we get back to base."

I flinched at the judgment in Tulip's narrowed eyes, the accusation of weakness she'd always tried to fix. My softness in a world that only rewarded the strong.

"Please," I said, prepared for the moment she'd push me. Shoot Buzz in the forehead. Rip away the dream I'd clung to for so many years: of one more night for us to talk, to look up at the stars. Pretending I could fly with him off into the sunset.

But, for once, Tulip listened. For once, she gave me grace. Likely seeing the secret I'd hidden for so long. The wedge I'd kept between us, always there, but never spoken.

She lowered her gun, and she pointed to my glider. "You take him," she said. "I'll follow behind." The implication being: if I tried to run away, if I took us off-course, she and her pistol would be right at our heels.

So, with Tulip watching over me, I scooped Buzz up, wrapped his arm around my shoulders, his musk and his warmth as familiar as ever. I lay him in my pod, squeezed beside him in the seat, his eyes shut, too weak to do much more than breathe. And together, we flew toward the base he'd abandoned. The base he'd never get to leave. Hoping, this time, I had made the right choice.

When I walked into his prison cell in the basement of the Dandelion, Buzz was in his bed. His leg clamped in a brace to heal the bones we'd recently set. His hair trimmed, cuts bandaged, shallow breath coming easy in the cell's filtered air.

He sat up as I entered, fell back into the pillow, his muscles still weakened from the pollen's near-paralysis. I noticed the smile lines creasing his cheeks, the crow's-feet near his eyes, my mouth filled with all the secret things I wanted to say, what I'd *dreamed* I would say, if I ever got the chance.

Instead, all I managed to whisper was, "I missed you."

Buzz smiled up at me, dragging me back to that day in the clearing, compressing twenty years into the blink of an eye, as if all the time I'd lost, all the blessings I'd lived—Tulip and Petal and the recent badge she'd earned, that I'd pinned to her uniform in the latest officer ceremony—had never even happened.

"I missed you, too," he said, his voice a bit groggy, a hint of excitement still just beneath the surface.

I smiled, didn't want to think of what would happen next: the trial that afternoon, in only a few hours; the inevitable guilty verdict; the punishment he'd earn—that *I* would have to inflict, as our senior-most officer. Two bullets to the head. A quick, simple death.

"I'm sorry," I said, even though I really wasn't. Would have burned every field and every flower to see him safe. "I shouldn't have brought you back here."

Buzz shook his head, and he reached for my hand, pulled me close. "I'm glad you did."

I sat beside him on the bed. Both of us knowing he'd never escape. The Dandelion's rules weighing heavy on our shoulders.

The silence settled in. He leaned into my arm, as if the bed were his pod, and the cell were that field, and the ceiling was a sky filled with twin violet suns that we could watch sinking into the distant horizon.

"Was it worth it?" he said, barely loud enough to hear.

I paused, closed my eyes. Knew he didn't mean the cell, or the rescue, or this moment. He meant the years in between. The years we'd spent alone.

"I . . . I think so," I said, still not quite sure. If I would *ever* be sure. If I would replay that day for the rest of my life, could ever mend the broken halves of what my life could have been.

None of which I said, my heart heavy with guilt, as we lay there together, and Buzz drifted into sleep.

Two hours later, it was time for us to go up.

Buzz limped along beside me, the pollen's numbing agents not yet faded from his bloodstream. But he didn't resist. He walked to the elevator, to his own execution, like he'd done everything else: confident, ready, with a great, goofy smile, like all his choices had been destined to lead him to this moment.

So different from the mountain of regrets I held now, with his trial and his death only moments away.

"It's OK," he said, leaning on my shoulder for balance. "I'm OK, we can do this." Lending me the strength I so desperately needed.

And yet, *could* I really do this? Could I look him in the eyes, raise a pistol to his forehead, watch his joy all leak out like his blood on the cold floor? Knowing, deep down, it was all my fault, and if I'd stayed, if I'd done what he'd asked me that day, none of this would have happened.

I watched as the elevator slowly took us up: past the prison cells, the bunkers, the Dandelion's main levels, all flashing by in front of us through the plexiglass screen. I held my finger over the button that would bring us to a stop. Only one floor away now. Where Tulip and the rest of my officers were waiting. My hand started to shake, breath tight in my chest. The choice I had to make again was close, *too* close. Duty or freedom. The choice I'd gone back to for twenty long years. What I wish I could have done.

What I could now make right.

The floor rushed past, and I lowered my hand, still trembling, to my side.

Buzz turned to face me, his smile now gone. "What are you doing?"

I still wasn't sure. Didn't know how it would end. Only knew it could destroy me, strip my title and badge. But at least he'd be safe. At least he'd be free: to live a life beneath the clouds, watch the suns on the horizon.

Our elevator stopped at the top of the shaft. The very highest floor. The hangar where a handful of gliders still remained.

I pulled Buzz, stumbling, to one of the parked pods. "You have to hurry," I said, swinging open the door. "They'll see we didn't stop. They'll catch the next elevator up."

Buzz moved jerkily, stiffened by the pollen. He strapped himself in, pulled a mask over his mouth, cranked the glider's rattling engine as I plugged in the coordinates: to a field by a mountain that was far, far away, where no one would ever find him.

But I didn't get in. I didn't squeeze beside him.

"Come with me?" he said, even though he knew the answer, knew I'd never be able to leave. Not with my wife and my daughter below, who still needed me here: to lead them, to *protect* them.

"Be careful out there," I said, before I swung shut the door. So that I couldn't change my mind, jump in and fly away like my younger self wished, still *screaming* for me to go.

But it was too late. The glider had already risen. It zipped from the hangar as the elevator door opened, as Tulip rushed over and shot at the wings, too far away to hit, and I watched Buzz leave me for the very last time.

Later that day, I was thrown into a prison cell.

Tulip didn't visit me, too angry at what I'd done. Undermining the cause we'd dedicated our lives to. The only one who came was Petal. She gave me water, snuck me jerky, pulled a chair up to the other side of my plexiglass cell. And she asked me why I'd done it, why I would risk my own life to save a man I hardly knew.

"He was special to me," I told her, still hiding the rest. Afraid of what she'd say, of who she'd tell, of how she'd *hate* me.

Petal, though, paused. She leaned into the glass. "Did you love him?" she said, her eighteen-year-old wisdom shining bright in her eyes. The same way she'd noticed—when she was just a little girl—how Tulip never kissed me, how we didn't seem as happy as we both should have been. Seeing things no one else cared enough to see. The truth of the world. The truth of who I *was*.

"I did," I said, still scared to admit it. "I . . . I *do*."

Silence. Neither one of us met the other's eyes.

Then, she left; she didn't come back to see me the next day. Alone in the dark and the cold and my regrets. Knowing she could pick through the words I'd kept hidden, and how she'd never forgive me.

Until, one night, the lights clicked back on. My cell door slid open. And Petal stood in front of me, a heavy bag over her shoulder, filled with vitamins and face masks and a canteen to filter rainwater. Anything she could steal from the Dandelion's bunkers. "Enough to last for a *whole month*," she said, giddy with excitement, the childlike joy of bending the rules. One of many things I'd taught her; one I hoped she never lost.

Then, she pushed me to the elevator and rushed me to the top, where the open door of a glider-pod was already prepped for me to climb into.

I spun around, wrapped her in a suffocating hug. But, young as she was, she hugged me back even stronger. "Go out and find him," she whispered. She kissed me on the cheek, strapped me into the pod, neither one of us brave enough to say the last goodbye.

And before I could stop her, she slammed shut the door. The pod engines roared, shot me out from the hangar, following the coordinates she'd plugged into the controls, my life and my family and my home far behind me.

I flew for three days. Away from the Dandelion. Toward the mountains and the suns on the distant horizon.

But I didn't see Buzz. Nothing around me but miles of yellow grass. He wasn't near the coordinates I'd plugged into his glider. He wasn't in the dozens of bee swarms I passed. He was lost. He was gone. He was never coming back.

I backtracked, whipped by the strengthening spring wind. Flew to the only other place I thought could be safe. The clearing where we'd first met. Still empty. Still stamped with a shallow ditch down the middle, from where my glider had crashed more than twenty years before.

I landed in the dirt. Tried to weather the storm, the walls of my glider-pod shaking from the wind. I wrapped my arms around my knees, braced myself for the window to shatter in front of me, the pollen to rush in and clog up my throat, lull me to a sleep from which I'd never wake up.

Thankfully, it didn't. When the wind died down and the rain turned to drizzle, the clouds began to part. The twin suns peeked out, violet and menacing and beautiful as ever. And with them came something I never expected. Something I thought I'd never get to see again.

Buzz, out in the dirt, standing next to his glider. His mask ripped off and his smile so bright, and my name on his lips as he screamed into the wind.

I jumped out of my pod, ran across the clearing. Didn't care if the bees or the flowers could see me, of what Tulip would say once she learned what I'd done. Only cared about Buzz as I crashed into his chest, and I wrapped him in a hug, and I whispered into his ear, *I found it, I* found *it*, all the world's happiness right there in my arms.

ABOUT THE AUTHOR

Ryan Cole is a speculative fiction writer who lives in Virginia with his husband and snuggly pug child. His work has appeared or is forthcoming in *Clarkesworld, PodCastle, Escape Pod, Cast of Wonders,* and *This Way Lies Madness* (Flame Tree Press), among others, and has been nominated for the Pushcart Prize.

Vwooom!

UCHECHUKWU NWAKA

The suit is too tight. Pinches just a little too uncomfortably around your neck, like phantom gnarly fingers constricting your windpipe. You swallow a lump. It's only nerves. A bead of sweat zigzags down the side of your face, distracting you from all the readings in your helmet's HUD. Your recently modified vertebral implants feel like a caterpillar crawling down your back. Skittering. Biting. Chewing.

You've not needed the augments since the Amadiohas were decommissioned. You think that you should have removed them. That's what they suggest at the rehabilitation home for the ex-pilots anyway. You only attend to humor Pa Ebube, but you know you'll never let go of the reinforced skeleton. Not with the power it brings you. How else would you have survived all those brawls in the Pits?

How else would you have been eligible for this trial flight into the Eye of Abstinence?

The cockpit is a glass coffin. The engine hums like the purr of a feline. A primal hunter stalking its prey. The vibrations seep into your bones. Your pupils dilate as the world stretches before you—concentric rings of white lights that form the tunnel of the accelerator gates. Electromagnetic fields pulse, and your heartbeat flutters. Your breath escapes in shallow puffs. The engine roars behind you, but you do not hear it over the rush of blood pounding against your eardrums. Your bloodstream is flooded with catecholamines.

It is the same feeling as being uplinked into the Amadioha—the fifteen-foot mechanical organism of utter destruction. When you swing your fist, the massive metallic limbs pierce through another mecha in an earsplitting explosion. Ideally, within the Amadioha, pilots are not supposed to see the pool of blood beneath the tanks they have trampled below their feet like steel ants. However, there is something different about your sync rate. Your tragic need to hyper-focus. Which means that you see the corpses of your enemies—once brothers, separated by tribe and prejudice—littered across former cityscapes, in a civil war labeled The Separation by poets who escaped conscription.

You still see the blood when you close your eyes.

It is why you don't blink as you stare into the darkness. The gullet *of the Eye.*

The war ended over a decade ago. The iron angels that crushed the Earth beneath their heels at the command of their faceless masters in the space stations suspended in the heavens have been turned to scrap. The pilots have long been left to fend for themselves. You trade one master for another. Champion of the Pits. You ignore messages from Pa Ebube and delete his holos before you can see the worry behind his eyes. The crow's feet that you've always known him to have. His silver hair has begun to seem thinner, but didn't everyone lose something in The Separation? The world is no longer like the days of your youth. Back when you started living in Pa Ebube's house, with his family of five. Your parents had died in a tribal terror attack, and somehow, he'd taken you in. Even with the economy tightening like a noose around the people's necks.

Not unlike the helmet around your head now. The hangman's noose around your neck.

He wants you to get a degree.

You dive into the etherspace for hours on that second-hand—maybe *fifth*-hand—headpiece, working on virtual workspace schoolwork. Most times, you're trying to pretend like you do not hear Aunty's discontent with Pa Ebube's decision to adopt you. So many credits are being spent on your education. Deep down, you believe her. Would it not be better for the household if you spent your time working as a salesboy in her restaurant, instead of wasting precious hours painting caricatures on a glorified Game Boy? If Pa Ebube chooses to funnel the money going into your art degree into Aunty's business, then everybody gains. After all, things are harder by the day with growing tensions. Insecurity. Tribal attacks. What would an orphaned artist have to offer, doing a job that any AI could?

Also, what does it matter if the thoughts originated in the razor-sharp tongue of Aunty's ire? They are yours now, no?

You lose your biometrics in an etherspace hack, subsequently losing your tuition. You have never been the best at handling criticism. You take the tragedy as a sign from God. The first of many.

The ship blasts forward. A fusiform needle of pure combustion power. The Gs press into you from all sides, and you're suddenly in that liminal plane of existence between being and not. Like a balloon, molecules stretching, bonds pulling at each other in hyperinflation—almost, but not yet bursting. While you rattle about in the cockpit, charges build along the jet's chassis. The tunnel supercharges the vessel.

Vwooom!

Your vision is replaced by a spectrum of light, blazing in electric streams past your irises. The world melts into nothingness. Your implants prevent you from dissolving into immaterial sludge as your ship pierces into deep space like a rail gun's beam.

Your thoughts are not so lucky.

You do not get invited to Pa Ebube's burial, but you hear of it. You scrape up some money and take a shuttle to *Altitude*. The space station is larger than you expect, and you end up missing the ceremony. You hope to run into Ebube or anybody from the family, but then, whether by a trick of the light or a cruel joke from God, you catch your reflection by a viewport. Your face has hardened with time, misshapen by bruises and eyes reddened by the alcohol that never completely leaves your system.

You hate the person that looks back at you.

Hate how different you seem in your baggy jacket with all its patches, compared with the denizens of *Altitude*. Their sleek suits and kaftans bear creases so sharp, it hurts your eyes. You wonder if this is a life you could have had. Post-Separation, all the job listings indicated degree holders. Inclusivity was the name of the game, but augmented ex-Amadioha pilots seemed to have trouble getting jobs.

Fitting in.

Maybe if you'd waited and gotten that degree, you wouldn't have to live in the scraplands planetside. Maybe you would be here in *Altitude*, with its climate systems and avant-garde culture. Instead, you had to join the war to make a statement to Aunty. That you were not just some charity case. It was never even about avenging your family, you realized; on one cold night, after you'd woken up from a blood-filled nightmare, drenched in sweat, muscles cramped from sleeping in your mecha's cockpit.

Aunty did not give two shits then, and neither did she now.

Your eyes fall on a holo-ad recruiting ex-pilots on *The Okafor-Westwood* station, past Saturn.

You realize that only Pa ever reached out. You remember all the messages. The holos. Asking whether you were safe. The prayers that fell on ears that rang with tinnitus from one brawl punch too many. For all the rest cared, you were crushed to death when one of the many skyscrapers fell. Why bother about them now?

What do you *want?*

Pa Ebube was your only anchor, and he is gone. You never even took the chance to thank him, and the realization

breaks

you.

The Eye of Abstinence shatters your ship into a zillion shards of infinity.

Probes first picked up the Eye twelve years back. An anomaly in space-time slowly expanding in the darkness of space. The anomaly rejects everything inorganic, but its parameters remain mostly measurable. Scientists theorize the existence of exotic matter within the Eye, but tests remain limited.

Or used to be, until the first daredevil pilot slammed into it and vanished.

*Sensors blare alarms over your suit as your world fractures in spectral fire. You have one job. Live long enough to look into the Eye and relay those observations back to the science megastation—*The Okafor-Westwood. *The compensation—a million credits—is always paid in advance. A last meal token of sorts, even though nobody knows what lies on the other side of the Eye. Be it rebirth or ruin, you have left behind a request to donate your money to any orphanages left on Earth. As the Late Pa Ebube Palliative Fund.*

As your silent, final "thank you" to the cold void.

ABOUT THE AUTHOR

Uchechukwu Nwaka is an Igbo medical student at University of Ibadan, Nigeria. His works have appeared in *PodCastle, Escape Pod, Fusion Fragment, FIYAH, Omenana, and Brittle Paper,* among others. He won the Locus Award for Best Novelette ("The Rainbow Bank", *Giganotosaurus*) in 2024. His work has also been a finalist for the Utopia Award and long-listed for a BSFA Award. When he's not writing short fiction or working on his new novella, he can be found reading manga, streaming TV shows, playing amateur volleyball, or trying to catch up with his endless schoolwork.

The Rebellion is Real: *1984* and *The Handmaid's Tale* in 2025

CARRIE SESSAREGO

Rebellious speculative fiction gives us works that provide a compelling combination of striking imagery and broad reach that become real-life tools for protestors today. One of these works is *1984*, a novel that gave us the language we needed to identify the tools that oppressive regimes use to control their subjects. Another is *The Handmaid's Tale*, which both as a novel and as a television show gave us powerful imagery to use as a form of resistance. Both novels explore strategies of oppression as well as resistance that are relevant today.

The novel *1984* was published by George Orwell in 1949. Although there have been several adaptations of the novel, most famously the movie version released in 1984, this essay concerns the novel exclusively. Set in a dystopian world, the novel depicts Winston, a low-level government official, as he tries to maintain a sense of self and autonomy in the face of overwhelming totalitarian forces.

In this world, the country of Oceania is locked in an endless and mutually destructive war with the rest of the world. Oceania is ruled by The Party under the leadership of a mysterious figure known as Big Brother. Every room in Oceania (or, at a minimum, London, the city in which the events of the book take place) is under constant surveillance through television screens and other equipment. Children are trained to spy on their parents, and adults spy on one another.

While some of the control of its citizens is physical, most of the control exerted by the government is psychological and involves the government's efforts to control its citizens' perception of reality. Citizens become accustomed to "The Ministry of Peace," which controls war, and "The Ministry of Love," which concerns torture. They are forced to read and repeat the slogans, "War is Peace," "Freedom is Slavery," and "Ignorance is Strength." Historical records and newscasts are altered to paint Big Brother in a wholly positive light. An example of the surrealism of life under Big Brother comes early in the book:

> *This was not illegal (nothing was illegal, since there were no longer any laws), but if detected it was reasonably certain that it would be punished by death, or at least by twenty-five years in a forced-labour camp.*

The forms of resistance displayed in *1984* are primarily inward—the battle to preserve one's sense of individuality in a world in which "Nothing was your own except the few cubic centimetres inside your skull." Winston begins his rebellion by committing "thoughtcrimes," entertaining thoughts that are out of alignment with the teachings of Big Brother. His rebellion escalates even further when he begins writing a diary.

When Winston and a woman named Julia begin a forbidden affair, it represents a massive escalation of rebellion. Sex is supposed to be a joyless exercise conducted for the purposes of procreation, not pleasure:

> *The aim of the party was not merely to prevent men and women from forming loyalties which it might not be able to control. Its real, undeclared purpose was to remove all pleasure from the sexual act . . . sexual intercourse was to be looked on as a slightly disgusting minor operation, like having an enema.*

Above all, Winston and Julia's affair is illicit because these emotions and these acts occur without permission. Their feelings for each other, emotional and sexual, exist beyond Big Brother. The energy they spend making love is energy not used toward The Party's goals. Their time together is spent where and when they believe no one can see them, and they feel things that Big Brother did not tell them to feel.

Julia is content to limit her rebellion to this affair, but Winston remains frustrated. He is thrilled when O'Brien, a colleague from work, promises to welcome him to a resistance movement called "The Brotherhood." Winston and Julia happily agree to do anything the Brotherhood might ask them to do, with one exception: they will not separate. There are many ways to interpret this in terms of the novel's themes, but one is that by demanding complete obedience in the total absence of information and input, The Brotherhood is acting no differently than Big Brother. Both demand not only physical but mental control. Even though Winston and Julia differ in their approaches to a larger resistance, they are both committed to choosing and controlling their own emotions and priorities instead of having those decisions foisted upon them.

O'Brien is eventually revealed to be a spy who imprisons and tortures Winston. He insists it's not enough for Winston to say what O'Brien wants him to say under torture. Rather, Winston must really, truly believe it. Winston swears that he will keep a little piece of his mind for himself. They can, he reasons, make him say or do anything, but in a small part of himself, he will still love Julia. When confronted with his worst fear in dreaded "Room 101," he screams. "Do it to Julia," and is then released, a broken man who only and truly loves Big Brother, having lost that small part of himself that he previously believed to be inviolable.

While the specifics of the world in *1984* are imaginary, Orwell based most of the tactics of Big Brother on real-world tactics from Nazi Germany and the Soviet Union under Joseph Stalin. For instance, both regimes professed a fanatical degree of nationalism and taught children to spy on and betray their own families. Orwell based the "Thought Police" and the tortures committed in The Ministry of Love on the Soviet People's Commissariat for Internal Affairs (NKVD), which was instrumental in carrying out The Great Purge under Stalin. Stalin's control of the press and all printed material also influenced Orwell's writing of Winston's job in The Ministry of Truth.

If there's anything *1984* teaches us, it's that those who control the language control the world. *1984* is interesting not only for its content as a novel, but for the way that content became part of the content of our own lives. The novel gifted us with a way of speaking about and thinking about totalitarianism that had not previously existed. Its language and its explanation of thought control techniques were so influential that many people have forgotten where they come from. While many books discussed the use of force, few had tackled the impact of propaganda, surveillance, and manipulation on "hearts and minds," a phrase first used by French colonialist forces in Vietnam in 1895.

Since being published, "Big Brother is watching you" has become a common way to refer to verified or suspected surveillance in real life. Instead of falling out of fashion, the phrase seems more relevant every year and is used to express concerns about, among other things, facial recognition software, social media, and artificial intelligence. In the United Kingdom, a group called Big Brother Watch campaigns against surveillance. Most bizarrely, a reality show called *Big Brother* that involves contestants being constantly monitored has run for twenty-six seasons in America alone (other countries have their own versions of this show).

1984 also introduced words like thoughtcrime, newspeak, unperson, doublespeak, memory hole, and facecrime. The term "memory hole" or "memory-hole" is used in computing and on the Internet in discussions about preserving digital information and knowledge. "Newspeak" became the name of a programming language. "Newspeak" is still used today by many political parties to describe language that is designed to limit the ability of people to express complex feelings or thoughts, which in turn is used to manipulate people into following a particular plan or agenda.

Finally, the novel, as well as other novels by George Orwell, sparked the term "Orwellian." This term describes a situation in which the sociopolitical atmosphere includes a feeling of being constantly watched, the presence of censorship, and tight control over language and what is presented as factual, as well as a sense of paranoia and dread. The word has been and continues to be deployed by both the political left and the political right.

More than any specific word, the novel has gifted us with an understanding of how language and control of language affect systems of oppression and resistance. The political Right in modern America has increased efforts to scrub libraries, textbooks, and websites of mentions of people and events from history that reflect the more painful aspects of America's past. Critical race theory has come under such virulent attack that many schools are unable to discuss issues like slavery, segregation, and discrimination at all, while books that depict these parts of our history, as well as issues around gender, religion, and class, are also pulled from the shelves.

The words from *1984,* like "newspeak," have been largely replaced by words like "wokeness," "fake news," "alternative facts," "internment," "antifa," and "witch hunt." Even though the words themselves are different, they serve the same purposes that words like "doublethink" and "unperson" served in *1984. 1984* demonstrates a use of language that allows us to recognize these actions as the acts of oppression that they are. Efforts by any government to rewrite the past and reframe the present are actions toward the future that O'Brien describes: "... a boot stamping on a human face—forever."

The Handmaid's Tale, written by Margaret Atwood in 1985, has also sparked debate and conversation since its publication. These conversations gained a new level when a television series loosely based on the novel premiered on Hulu in 2017. This year, *The Handmaid's Tale* is in its final season, having moved far beyond the content of the novel, and Handmaids continue to appear at protest events across the globe.

The novel is told in the form of journal recordings made by a woman known only as Offred. Offred is held against her will in the Republic of Gilead, a dictatorial and patriarchal theocracy that has overthrown the government of the United States of America. Under this regime, women are subject to a variety of restrictive laws. Adult women are divided into categories. They may be Wives (the wives of high-ranking military officers), Marthas (domestic servants), Aunts (the trainers and overseers of Handmaids), Econowives (wives of lower-status men), or Handmaids.

Handmaids are fertile women deemed unsuitable for marriage because they have broken one of Gilead's laws, often retroactively. They are assigned to the homes of Commanders and ritually raped over three consecutive nights during their ovulation every month. If they become pregnant, the baby is taken from them after birth and given to the Commander and his Wife, after which the Handmaid is assigned to a new household. If they fail to conceive after a certain number of attempts, they are moved to a new household, or they may be sent to "The Colonies" (work camps) where they will become "unwomen" (a word borrowed from *1984).* The Handmaids' names are assigned on a temporary basis that reflects their placement. The narrator is called "Offred" because she is assigned to Fred Waterford and is thus "of Fred."

In the television show, her real name is given as June. The television show quickly moves beyond the events of the novel and details June's attempts to rescue her daughter and to overthrow Gilead. The world and the characters are greatly expanded as we move beyond June's point of view and see life beyond the borders of Gilead.

June's initial rebellious actions are personal ones. Like Winston in *1984*, she keeps an illegal diary. She makes multiple attempts to escape from Gilead. She also engages in more subtle forms of rebellion. Instead of passively accepting her new identity as a Handmaid, she keeps her identity as June alive, even if she can only do so in her own mind. She memorializes people who have died, she keeps her memories of her past alive, she persists in trying to reunite with her daughter.

June very consciously and deliberately keeps herself "June," a woman with her own desires and thoughts outside of what Gilead wants her to feel and think. June and Winston are very different people, but they are similar in their dedication to preserving "the few cubic centimetres inside your skull." Like Winston in *1984*, she rebels by daring to enjoy sex and love (in an illegal relationship with Nick).

At the beginning of season two, June's latest escape resulted in not only her capture but in devastating punishments wreaked upon people who helped her, as well as complete innocents who are punished while June is forced to watch. It is this weight of guilt that Aunt Lydia uses to finally convince June that there is no June. While June is "not worthy," Offred is "innocent." This episode lacks a voice-over, showing that June has surrendered even her innermost thoughts.

Her biggest act of rebellion in the second episode of season two is to refrain from reporting her vaginal bleeding, a sort of suicide by inaction (she is pregnant at this time). The only reason that she is able to come back to herself is her admiration for her as-yet unborn baby, who survives the medical crisis and who June calls "tough." Even though this emotional journey from internal resistance to capitulation and back again is brief, it is important because it shows the strength that even invisible internal resistance requires.

By the beginning of Season Three, June's priorities have shifted. Having smuggled Nichole to Canada, she chooses to stay in Gilead in hopes of saving Hannah. While saving Hannah is always her primary goal, June becomes increasingly committed to saving others by bringing down Gilead as a whole. Unlike the regime in *1984*, Gilead is new and fragile and has not yet seized full control of people's minds and hearts, which means broader resistance is possible. While internal rebellion remains important, increasing focus is given to outward, violent, organized resistance.

Neither the novel nor the show shies away from depicting the consequences of rebellion in a totalitarian society. Both include public executions, beatings, mutilations, and the threat of being sent to the deadly Colonies. In the series, June is frequently forced to watch others being killed or punished for her actions, and she is told that other loved ones, including her daughter, will be harmed if she transgresses. All of these tactics, including public executions, control of public narratives, carefully controlled outlets for rage, and an atmosphere of paranoia and confusion are shared with real-life regimes and with *1984*.

The Handmaid's Tale is interesting because it has inspired very specific real-life resistance to efforts to control the reproductive lives of women as well as those of trans men, nonbinary people, and all individuals who have wombs. Handmaids in the show are forced to wear red dresses and cloaks as well as white bonnets. Beginning in May 2017, people dressed as Handmaids began appearing in public settings across the globe to advocate for women's rights. Protestors dressed as Handmaids have appeared across the United States of America as well as other countries, including Israel, Northern Ireland, the Republic of Ireland, Great Britain, Argentina, Croatia, Poland, and Canada.

The costumes from the television show have proved to be highly suited for protest work. The imagery is striking, simple, immediately recognizable, and easily replicated. It can be suitable for hot or cold weather, and the hoods help hide the face. Some protestors add a step of dramatically removing their Handmaid robes at a predetermined moment during the protest event, symbolizing their rejection of patriarchal rule.

However, adoption of Handmaid robes as protest is not uncomplicated. Both the novel and the show have been criticized for how they handle race, and Handmaid-costumed protestors are disproportionately white. In some cases, protestors have been criticized by others for dressing as Handmaids. While the imagery serves as a warning: take action now, before the world of the novel/series happens here! This suggests that the danger to women is a new thing ominously looming ahead, instead of a set of very real discriminatory practices that have existed around the world in both the past and the present. This ignores the very real past and immediate present in which people of color have been subjected to some version of every restriction imposed by Gilead.

Both *1984* and *The Handmaid's Tale* use a speculative fiction framework to discuss real-life forms of oppression and resistance. Both challenge us to reckon with the past and hold fast to our humanity in a darkening present. Both novels include afterwords that describe their respective dystopias in the past tense. By using the insights provided by these stories, perhaps we too can resist and regulate oppression and tyranny to the past tense.

ABOUT THE AUTHOR

Carrie Sessarego is the resident "geek reviewer" for *Smart Bitches, Trashy Books,* where she wrangles science fiction, fantasy romance, comics, movies, and non-fiction. Carrie's first book, *Pride, Prejudice, and Popcorn: TV and Film Adaptations of Pride and Prejudice, Wuthering Heights, and Jane Eyre,* was released in 2014. Her work has been published in *Interfictions Online, Pop Matters: After the Avengers, The WisCon Chronicles Vol. 9, Invisible 3, Clarkesworld Magazine,* and two volumes of *Speculative Fiction: The Year's Best Online Reviews, Essays and Commentary.* She spends her time wrangling her husband, daughter, dog, and three cats.

Women, Technology, and the Future: A Conversation with Brenda Cooper

ARLEY SORG

Brenda Cooper was born in Encino, CA, and grew up in Hidden Hills. "I'm a classic California 'Valley Girl' who moved south to Orange County at ten. Then I spent most of High School ditching class to surf beaches like Doheny and Redondo Beach, and Trestles that the Beach Boys sang about." Cooper started reading early and remembers reading the newspaper every day with her dad. "When I went to kindergarten, they gave me a picture book. I came home furious, saying I never wanted to go to school again if they weren't willing to teach me anything." Around the same age, she started writing poetry.

Cooper started working at age twelve, harvesting eggs and delivering them to houses around the neighborhood—on a unicycle. "At one point, while I was a teenage runaway, I worked on a worm farm in Eugene, Oregon. We captured night crawlers with flashlights at midnight and dug in rabbit poop for red wrigglers at noon. This only lasted a few months. I liked it, though."

Cooper earned a BA in management information systems at California State University, Fullerton. "Dad said he'd pay for college if I didn't get an English degree. He said I needed to pay bills, and the humanities wasn't going to do that. For context, he's a rocket scientist, and he was right. At the time, I was a single teenage mom with a one year old. I have paid all our bills. My son is now a forty-five-year-old successful firefighter." Over the years, she stayed involved in writing communities, often learning and developing writing skills along the way. She helped Steven Barnes with his *Lifewriting* classes, studied with Dean Wesley Smith and Kristine Kathryn Rusch, and attended Patrick Swenson's Rainforest Writers Retreat many times. Even after her professional and personal successes, including already publishing a number of books, Cooper returned to education in her fifties, earning her MFA from Stonecoast. "I had SO MUCH FUN. Loved it. I got to study with Martín Espada, this fiery, brilliant Puerto Rican poet. When he performed his poetry, he utterly owned the room. I also got to work with Debra Marquart, Rick Bass, Elizabeth Hand, Nancy Holder, and more."

Cooper's work—nonfiction, poetry, and fiction—began appearing in publications in the early 2000s. Some of her earliest published fiction pieces were cowritten with Larry Niven, such as debut short story "Ice and Mirrors" (*Asimov's Science Fiction*, February 2001). It wouldn't be long before she was selling fiction as a soloist. In 2002, she had the story "Recovery" in *The Salal Review*, and in 2003, "Linda's Dragon" was published in *Analog Science Fiction and Fact*, as well as "Touches the Earth" in anthology *Sun in Glory and Other Tales of Valdemar* (DAW). She was a Sturgeon finalist for 2004 *Analog* story "Savant Songs."

In 2005, with a fair number of short stories in respected magazines and anthologies, Cooper's debut novel *Building Harlequin's Moon* came out with Tor, again cowritten with Niven. Her solo debut *The Silver Ship and the Sea* was published by Tor in 2007, earning her a Golden Duck nomination and an Endeavour Award win. She also received a Philip K. Dick nomination and won another Endeavour Award for 2015 novel *Edge of Dark* (Pyr). To date, Brenda Cooper has over eighty short stories out, two collections, and thirteen novels.

Writing has always been central to Brenda Cooper's life. "When I was in Junior High, I won the seventh-grade skateboarding contest. I was the only girl who entered. Other than that, I've had various awards in my tech career. There is one story worth telling. A major tech magazine gave me an award in front of at least a few hundred people at a tech conference. I was pleased. Then I stopped in a Barnes & Noble on the way home and picked up Gardner Dozois' Year's Best. And there, I found one of my stories had made it to his honorable mention list. Not into the book, not into his overview, just into the long list at the back of the book. I was so happy I sat down in the middle of the aisle and bawled."

Brenda Cooper lives in WA state with her wife, Toni, and six dogs. She describes herself as having "multiple careers" as a writer, a technologist, and a futurist. She is currently the IT Director for Lease Crutcher Lewis, a local construction company. Her latest book is collection *When Mothers Dream: Stories*, due this month from Fairwood Press.

You've been publishing fiction since the early 2000s and have a good number of novels out, as well as a slew of short stories. What is writing to you, and has the personal meaning of writing changed over time?

Writing is like air. If I don't write for a while, I get itchy. I almost never get writer's block (except once; see below). I don't have nearly enough time (for anything—not enough time to write or read or visit with people I love or to travel), so I can't wait to see what happens when I have more time to write.

I wrote when I was young, when I was a teenager, and then started again when I was thirty-seven. The time in between, from when I had my son to when he turned eighteen, I mostly wrote about how I wanted to write. There was a long stretch of time when I didn't give myself permission to write. I'd gone and had a kid, and now I had to be a mom, and that meant I had to focus on everything except what I wanted. Now, years later, I know that was hooey. But I think that's how I made it through motherhood. I mean, I had serial children. Toni had a six year old when I met her, and Katie didn't slow me down. But I was nineteen and scared when I had my son, and older and more confident when I met Katie. That's a long-winded way to say I've written most of my life, except for one very long stretch when I was doing something else important.

How did you first get into writing—and how (as well as why) did you transition to writing seriously, as an endeavor with purpose?

I already told the story of my long hiatus. During that time, I *did* work with Steven Barnes on *Lifewriting*. I did write a bit, but mostly I used my first lessons from Steve to prepare to write, and to start to believe I could chase my dreams. *Lifewriting* also goosed me into moving to WA state. Steve helped me learn to accept rejection as food for growth.

After my son David turned eighteen, I gave myself permission to go back to school, and I took a creative writing class at the local community college in Longview, WA. Since creative writing was homework, I could do it. I got lucky. The instructor LOVED words, and even though he didn't write or read SF, he thought it was fine that I loved it. His name was Joe, and he was about sixty, married to a potter, and he had a letterpress in his basement. And did I mention that he loved words? Joe loved words. It was like finding a member of my tribe.

Now, of course, the fandom community is my tribe, and many of my best friends are writers.

One thing that's changing is I can smell the barn. I have maybe two decades of good writing left? Three if I figure out how to stop eating processed food? So it feels like time to up my game, lean in, and do more.

What do you feel are your most important observations about the publishing industry?

Tough question. Large publishers can break you out, they can make you and give you an easier shot at the gold ring. They also won't hesitate to crush you, casually, maybe without even noticing they stepped on you. I might have PTSD regarding large publishers. Smaller publishers are far more supportive, and it's more of a mutual work to find some level of success. But they don't reach as far. They're a harder road to bestseller lists or awards.

Mostly, I think what I've learned is to never depend on this industry to eat. Do it because you love it, because the people are awesome, and the work is the best in the world, but don't rely on the publishing industry to pay your mortgage.

Does short fiction play a very different role for you than longer works, do you have a different relationship to shorter forms, or do both work in similar ways for you?

I love both. For me, they are different.

Other than an annual and very fun foray into Mercedes Lackey's Valdemar, most of my short work is science fiction. Short SF lets me give readers an image of the future we're choosing to create, maybe to provide some fresh way to think about it. It's often about a single idea. One of my most successful stories, "The Robot's Girl," came from a two-paragraph article I read about robots raising children in Japan. "Biology at the End of the World" is about creating life and how we could be pushed into playing God. It came from fretting about reefs I watched deteriorate in Mexico and reading Yuval Noah Harari's book, *Homo Deus*. Lastly, a lot of my short fiction comes from anthology invites, so there's a bit of a prompt to start the work. My brain likes that structure, as long as the prompt isn't too restrictive.

Long fiction requires a deeper lean into character and more complex worldbuilding, both of which I truly love. I've done more short work than long the last few years, but that's mostly about time. I've had family and work things that mattered to attend to, and novels are hard to leave and come back to, while short work can be drafted in a day or two and then edited as time allows.

When Mothers Dream: Stories is your fourth collection. When you think of your earlier collections, Beyond the Waterfall Door, Cracking the Sky, and Stories of Fremont's Children, what sets this book apart for you?

Beyond the Waterfall Door is set in a magical version of the Sawdust Festival in Laguna Beach, CA. I worked there for a summer or two and had some seriously interesting experiences. This was me working through those, and it's very early writing. I haven't reread those in decades, but I suspect they are brave, creative, and clunky stories. It was also an attempt at self-publishing, where I paid a typesetter and an editor for the art and probably made back pennies on the dollar. Call it a life lesson. Luckily, while my heart depends on this career, the roof over my head doesn't. I may have sold ten copies.

Stories of Fremont's Children is set in one of my far-future series that starts with *The Silver Ship and the Sea*. *The Silver Ship* was my first solo novel and my first award-winning work. The series and the stories explore prejudices based on differences; in this case, genetically engineered superpowers. The stories can be read without the novels, and some were published separately. One, "The Hebras and the Demons and the Damned," came out in *Analog* first, and then in *Year's Best SF 16*, edited by David G. Hartwell and Kathryn Cramer.

Cracking the Sky is earlier work. I love some of the stories in there. I think it's held up fine, and readers who like this collection might enjoy it. *When Mother's Dream: Stories* was originally meant to be a sort of follow-on collection modeled on *Cracking the Sky*. But strange things happen on the way to the printed page.

When I set out to collect my most recent work, I noticed it was almost exclusively about women. About how we develop relationships, how we deal with adversity, how we feel about each other and the world. That felt critical. So, this came together as a book where every story is about or by women, and most of them are also about our relationship with the natural world in some ways. This collection offers a counterpoint to the very male-oriented stories of technical utopia that Sam Altman and Satya Nadella are telling us. I'm fascinated with technology, and see it as a tool, even a great tool. But it will not save us. We must save ourselves, and we can do that by transforming how we see each other and the world around us.

The earliest publication date in this book is "In Their Garden" (originally published in Asimov's in 2009). What is interesting about this piece, what made it a story that you wanted new readers to see?

"In Their Garden" is a hopeful story that explores the possibility of rebuilding what we are in the process of destroying. It was written as a stand-alone story, but readers wanted more and said so. That led to me writing *POST*, a coming-of-age novel that came out from eSpec Books. Readers who like "In Their Garden" might enjoy *POST*.

Looking at the selections, ranging from 2009 to new, original works, what do you see as the themes or concerns that you often come back to?

I write about nature and our relationship, responsibility, and connection to it a lot. This book is about women, and quite a bit about our Southern Resident Killer Whales, a set of three orca family pods that are in extreme danger of extinction. Some of the stories are also about technology, and pretty much all of them are about the future. This collection of stories may be the one that is most representative of me as a human, of what I have to bring to the party that we're all attending on this beautiful planet.

This book also offers readers six original poems. What is your approach to writing poetry, and how would you describe this set of poems?

I hadn't originally intended to include poetry, but I woke up one morning thinking I should, so I did.

Poetry was my first writing love. Even though I left it behind for decades and followed the siren song of stories, I reconnected to poetry with my MFA. I've really enjoyed writing more of it lately. There are also so many—so many—highly emotional moments in this whirlpool of change we're living through right now. Poetry is the perfect thing to drop into morning pages or scribble down when something hits me particularly hard.

A lot of the poetry I chose to include is about the orcas. It's all about the changes we are part of, and the warped future we're creating with our greed-based economics. The book ends on a poem about the burning world and how it feels to be enveloped by the smoke of our own stupidity.

The most recent stories here are "Solastalgia Meets the Alps" (Anthropocene, December 2022) and "Out of Ash" (Slate, May 2022). What can you tell us about these stories without giving too much away?

"Solastalgia Meets the Alps" came about because the term solastalgia (climate grief) resonates really hard in my core. I learned the word (new words are always cool!) and decided to write about it. Then . . . well . . . there is a fantastical machine that just needed to be written about. Lastly, it's also a story about being a working mom.

Slate's *Future Tense* is curated by Center for Science and the Imagination at Arizona State University. I've done so much work for and with them, they are almost chosen family. They particularly wanted a story about climate mitigation. "Out of Ash" became the seed for two or three other stories and an entire novel. "Out of Ash" is from a fictional WA state governor's viewpoint. I spent about twenty-five years working in local government, and it was full of people who cared for the community. It's a largely thankless job. Planning for and supporting cities is hard work, full of compromises and creativity. I wrote "Out of Ash" partly to show the positive side of government. So many people firmly believe all government is corrupt, self-dealing, and rather awful. Sometimes for good reasons, mind you. But most local government officials are doing hard work, struggling uphill through rivers of hatred, mistrust, and misplaced hope that change can be avoided.

You also gift the reader with a handful of stories original to the collection. Are there things that tie them together, or elements that may surprise readers who are familiar with your work?

"Annalee of the Orcas" and the title story, "When Mothers Dream," are both pretty much magical realism, which isn't really something I usually write. I love them both, but I expect they won't be what readers expect from me. So, I hope people enjoy them.

If you'd love for readers to look at two stories in this collection, what would you want them to be, and why?

"Her Granddaughters' Teachers" (new in this collection) talks about one of the more insidious risks of AI—which is that we perhaps come to enjoy working with AI too much, and that we might *like* the harm it does to us. It doesn't read like a horror story. It's calm and understated, really, and even presents itself partly as being about something else entirely. But it should trouble readers' dreams. AI is here, it's fascinating, it's growing fast, it's going to help us in many ways. But the risks should in no way be underestimated. They're real. And they're existential.

"Maybe the Monarchs" makes audiences bawl. I've read it out loud three times at conventions. Every time, the audience cried. I used to write mostly hopeful fiction, and I suppose I still will. Often, anyway. Some of these stories *are* hopeful. But sometimes the feeling a story wants the reader to take away is something sadder and more contemplative. I've done a lot of work to try and write well enough to invoke real feelings in readers, and this story does that, at least when read to people in groups.

Is there anything else you'd like Clarkesworld readers to know about you, your work, or When Mothers Dream: Stories?

The beautiful cover art by Rachel Byler represents the magic of found resonances. It's not commissioned for this book; I found it in an ad for her Etsy site. But the moment I saw it, I wanted it for the cover. I'm so pleased she let me buy the rights to use it here. It's a perfect illustration for "Annalee of the Orcas." I encourage readers who are interested in this book to go look at, and buy, Rachel's art.

ABOUT THE AUTHOR

Arley Sorg is an associate agent at kt literary. He is a two-time World Fantasy Award Finalist and a two-time Locus Award Finalist for his work as co-Editor-in-Chief at *Fantasy Magazine*. Arley is also a SFWA Solstice Award Recipient, a Space Cowboy Award Recipient, and a finalist for two Ignyte Awards. Arley is senior editor at *Locus*, associate editor at both *Lightspeed* & *Nightmare*, a columnist for *The Magazine of Fantasy and Science Fiction* and an interviewer for *Clarkesworld*.

Tactical Ballgowns and Genre Turduckens: A Conversation with Fran Wilde

ARLEY SORG

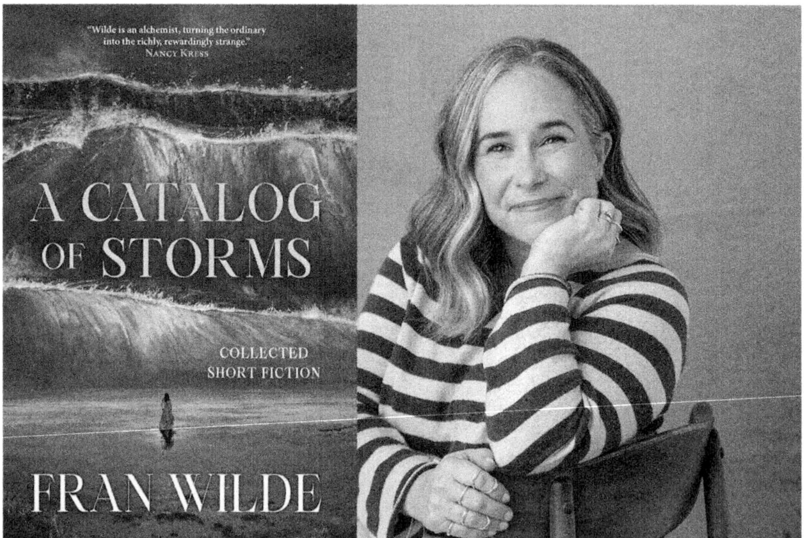

Fran Wilde was born in Philadelphia, PA. She spent many summers traveling back and forth from Philadelphia to Hopkinsville, KY. She began to read and write early on, and storytelling was a tradition in her family's household. She spent extensive time in the library, eventually discovering bookstores and all they had to offer. Her family kept classics as well as engineering books and other nonfiction texts, but Wilde went out of her way to explore science fiction.

In high school, Fran Wilde studied art and learned to design jewelry. She went to the University of Virginia and earned an English degree, studying writing and literature with an emphasis on poetry, as well as on Milton and eighteenth-century literature. She earned an MFA in poetry from Warren Wilson College and later earned another master's at the University of Baltimore in information architecture and interaction design. In 2011, Wilde attended Viable Paradise, followed by Taos Toolbox in 2012.

Fran Wilde has been publishing poetry since the nineties. She made a splash in genre fiction with short stories "Everlasting" and "Everyone Loves a Hero" in *Daily Science Fiction* in 2011, followed by "Without" in *Nature* in 2012. This was just the beginning: she has over fifty short stories published at a range of notable venues, and has racked up extensive accolades, including Nebula, World Fantasy, and Hugo awards finalist and Eugie winner "Clearly Lettered in a Mostly Steady Hand" (*Uncanny* 9-10/2017); as well as Locus, Nebula, and Hugo awards finalist "A Catalog of Storms" (*Uncanny* 1-2/2019).

Wilde's longer fiction has similarly received a wide range of recognition. For example, debut novel *Updraft* was published by Tor in 2015, launching the Bone Universe series. *Updraft* was a Nebula and Dragon awards finalist, won a Compton Crook Award, and secured Wilde an Andre Norton Nebula Award. Wilde has published several novels so far, including Locus Award finalist *Horizon* (Tor 2017) as well as Lodestar finalist and Andre Norton Nebula Award winner *Riverland* (Amulet 2019).

Other adventures include working as a sailing instructor, programmer, web designer, and more. Fran Wilde has taught at Vermont College of Fine Arts and St. Mary's College of Maryland. She was also the director of the genre fiction MFA concentration at Western Colorado University. In 2022, she cofounded and still coedits digital magazine *The Sunday Morning Transport*, which has earned her another World Fantasy finalist nod—in the Special Award, Non-Professional category—as well as a Locus Award finalist spot for Best Editor.

Fran Wilde lives in Maryland with her family. Collection *A Catalog of Storms* is due from Fairwood Press this month, and novel *A Philosophy of Thieves* is due from Erewhon next month.

You earned an MFA in poetry and later went on to teach and run MFA programs. A number of notable SFF authors have earned MFAs, but some have talked about difficult experiences with programs or have mentioned instructors who frowned on SFF. What are your thoughts about MFAs specifically for up-and-coming genre writers?

I did get my first master's in poetry (second one is in information architecture and interaction design)! I studied poetry with Heather McHugh, Eleanor Wilner, Larry Levis, Joan Aleshire, and Marianne Boruch (as well as Rita Dove, undergrad) at Warren Wilson College.

I am still close with many in my MFA cohort, and we cheer each other on, no matter what field we're working in. That, plus engaging in a close study of language and structure, was one of the joys of doing an MFA.

I think there's more willingness to encourage speculative writers in many MFA programs now—and that's a wonderful thing.

The best advice I can give to anyone considering an MFA, beyond using the time to read widely and stay curious, is to look at the structure of the program and make sure it works for you, as well as talking to recent grads and current students. You can get a good feel for what the program's like on the ground that way, which is important, as it is a big investment of time, energy, and money.

As well, knowing a bit about who is teaching at a particular program is useful—if you see a number of speculative writers on faculty, you'll have a good hint that your writing will be supported and nurtured, as well as your reading material, and your cohorts' interests.

You attended Viable Paradise and Taos Toolbox and have probably done a fair amount of teaching at some of the major SFF workshops. What are your recommendations to newer authors considering putting time, energy, and money into genre workshops?

VP and Taos Toolbox, and programs like them, including Writing Excuses and Futurescapes (where I often teach, and am co-keynoting with my agent Andrea Somberg this fall), are another excellent way to connect with craft and community simultaneously.

My advice: Read widely, stay curious, and know that your fellow writers are part of your community. Writing isn't *Highlander*—there can be many writers, and many kinds of success. Don't go in expecting to sell a story or get an agent—that's not what workshops are for. Go into a workshop environment with a willingness to learn many things, from different workshop methods and new writing techniques that might work for you, to meeting others who may become your colleagues, and maybe even long-term critique partners, is a very good way to set yourself up for an excellent experience.

Shorter answer: It's not just about having your work critiqued. It's about community and craft.

With all that said, you do not need a workshop or an MFA to be a writer! They're very useful for some, but they aren't for everyone, nor are they a requirement for the field! Reading widely and closely, writing, iterating, failing, trying again? That's the job.

Does having a foundation in poetry inform your writing, particularly your short fiction, or are they very separate modalities that don't really impact each other?

Poetry absolutely informs my writing. Poetry expects concision and play, and for words (and the sounds of words, and the multiple meanings of words) to do more than one thing at a time. That feeds my fiction and my editing processes for short fiction and long.

You've been coediting **The Sunday Morning Transport** ***with Julian Yap for several years now. Has editing short fiction changed anything about your own writing?***

Hah. It has occasionally meant less time to write, certainly. And it's meant amazing conversations about fiction with so many writers and readers. I wouldn't give that up for the world. Working with authors on their stories—from Will Alexander and A.R. Capetta, to Thomas Ha, David Bowles, and Kat Howard, just to name a few!—is a highlight of my day, and has been going on for four years now.

A Catalog of Storms ***is your first short fiction collection, following 2021 poetry collection*** **Clock Star Rose Spine**. ***What do you see as the role of collections for authors as well as for publishing—what makes them important?***

Collections are a great way to look at a body of work, I think. Also, I am a terrible forgetter of my own work sometimes, and gathering stories into a collection is fun because I get to discover it all again . . . (see below).

What did you learn through the process of collecting your short stories; or what surprised you?

There was definitely a lot of "HUH. I DID WRITE THAT," which was funny. See above. I was surprised how much horror was involved. And how many cross-genre stories there were—even from very early on. I admittedly think birds and storms (and weather in general) are great, and that setting can be a character. But I also think class, disability, and technology show up in my stories in a variety of ways—more than I expected.

Catalog offers fourteen stories that originally appeared in an assortment of publications, from Asimov's to Weird Tales. Are there a few entries here that may challenge readers in some ways?

Aren't stories supposed to challenge and engage readers in many different ways?

When it first came out, "Clearly Lettered in a Mostly Steady Hand" seemed to be one of those very challenging stories. I very definitely remember reading it for the first time at ICFA and, when I finished, looking up to a silenced room. That had never happened to me before, and I got very nervous and felt like I'd done something wrong. Then my friend, John Chu said, "Well, THAT was very different from you!" And everyone clapped, *finally*. The truth is, that story was very different because it cut very close to the bone as I unpacked disability themes and experiences—including anger and loss of agency/return of agency. John was absolutely right—that was very different for me! I don't often feel comfortable being angry, and this structure—a guided tour of different rooms in a cabinet of curiosities, one that used the second person to discomfiting effect on purpose, was a challenge because I was aware from the beginning that some might find that particularly uncomfortable. So yes, that one. I've been heartened by the ongoing reads of that story, and how it keeps reappearing in different places—and I'm very glad I took those risks!

"The Midway"—which I wrote for Ellen Datlow—is a novella that takes place in the dark unknown space beneath a familiar vacation place, along a seaside boardwalk. That combination of the monstrous and the whimsical is something I like to return to in different ways—in "Building Migration #1," "A Catalog of Storms," and "My Cloak of Keys," as well. That last one is about a small god of the dead who rescues the pets of the living. That kind of thing.

Which stories in this book were the ones that were harder to write, or for which you had to dig even deeper than usual?

"The Rain Remembers What the Sky Forgets" was really hard. I knew what I wanted to try with the story, and I could hear the characters just fine, but I kept running up against the story not story-ing, until I figured out what the structure needed to be. When I realized it was a tale told in letters and articles and found objects (quite literally), it all clicked. It's difficult to remember, when you've finished a story and it works, how difficult it can be to start. (I totally remember how hard this one was.)

You also have A Philosophy of Thieves coming up, with plans for a sequel. What was the initial inspiration for this book, and how did the story change or transform over time?

I initially wrote a short story where a family of entertainers is hired to rob a ball, so that another character can impress everyone with how wealthy he is based on how much he could afford to lose, and the first scene became the ballroom scene in "A Philosophy of Thieves." That short story was for a workshop with Gregory Frost, and he kept nudging me about where the book was—until I expanded and explored a world where that kind of entertainment might exist. The real world seems to be rising to meet that moment, a little bit—which is pretty weird.

The big transformations came when more voices and depth developed the plot(s) and all the interlocking heists, plus when I brought in more biotech that's tied to security, evolved the city's feed (a social network that is part Nextdoor, part YouTube, part Tumbler, part public access TV, and part functioning the way rumor does in George Eliot's *Middlemarch*). I also expanded on issues of ownership, inheritance, agency, and the fantastical elements of the wealthy enclave. But through it all, the Canarviers have been a troupe of entertainers caught up in a world where, as Daxian Canarvier says in one of his finer moments, "history was what the wealthy made happen to the poor."

Thieves is described as "Leverage meets Parasite meets Six of Crows," and includes "a high-stakes Grand Heist." What do you see as the thing that readers love about heist stories and thieves, why is it such a powerful and enduring trope?

The thing I love about heists (your mileage may vary!) is how much the structure of the narrative invites the reader in as a participant. We know how the gig is supposed to go off, because we are a witness to the plan. So we can see it going wrong when it does (and it definitely does), and how the characters work together to fix things. As well, the righting of wrongs aspect of many heists has a great feeling, even as the sleight of hand and daring exploits get more sleight and more daring.

What are the things that make your approach to the heist story different and interesting, or uniquely you? Are there things that Fran Wilde fans will find familiar in this book, as well as a few things that may surprise them?

Well, there's a tactical ballgown: a programmable fabric and a very talented seamstress makes Roosa Canarvier's outfit highly useful. It's also filled with pockets, *of course.*

There's a genre turducken of science fictional world on the outside and fantastical gaslamp mystery on the inside, with fan groups cheering on various players. And the multigenerational cast. There are surprises (I hope) throughout as far as what's really going on, and definitely issues of class, environment, and families found and inherited.

The main characters are the Canarviers, a group of thieves and artists. What can you tell us about a few of the most important characters, and what do you love most about them?

Roosa (Roo): Torn between two worlds; highly competent in both. Having to choose between them is tearing her apart.

Daxian (Dax): Thinks he should be in charge of the heists. Definitely not a great idea.

King Canarvier: Father to Dax and Roosa. Keeping way more secrets than anyone knows. When he is captured, the family could fall apart. Dax and Roo are determined to find him.

Mason Graves: Not quite the well-heeled gentleman he wants to be, definitely lucked into his biotech security company, hopes to ask the richest girl in town to marry him, if he can keep his background under wraps. He has a ring in his pocket and thieves in his house. What could possibly go wrong?

Evangeline Benford, Sam Benford: The aforementioned richest girl in town and her very protective father. Much more to them than meets the eye.

What, for you, is A Philosophy of Thieves about? What is the heart of the story?

Dax would say it's the Dazzle. Roo would insist it was the tech. King would say it is the history and art of the craft.

You have several novels out, as well as novellas. What are the things you've learned through writing book after book that you brought into writing A Philosophy of Thieves?

That every book is new—an open door into new ways to look at the world. Writing each book means actively thinking about and connecting so many elements—characters, myth, vibes, wonder, adventure, science, meaning—and I love doing it.

Is there anything else you'd like Clarkesworld readers to know about you, your work, A Philosophy of Thieves, or A Catalog of Storms?

Thank you for the wonderful interview, Arley! Someday, I'll sell Neil a zombie story. (JUST KIDDING.)

You can find me at franwilde.net, @fran_wilde on Instagram and Bluesky, and Patreon (https://www.patreon.com/c/franwilde). And out in the world—definitely find me in the bookstores!

ABOUT THE AUTHOR

Arley Sorg is an associate agent at kt literary. He is a two-time World Fantasy Award Finalist and a two-time Locus Award Finalist for his work as co-Editor-in-Chief at *Fantasy Magazine*. Arley is also a SFWA Solstice Award Recipient, a Space Cowboy Award Recipient, and a finalist for two Ignyte Awards. Arley is senior editor at *Locus*, associate editor at both *Lightspeed* & *Nightmare*, a columnist for *The Magazine of Fantasy and Science Fiction* and an interviewer for *Clarkesworld*.

Editor's Desk: The Future of Dealing with AI Submissions

NEIL CLARKE

While I was at Readercon last month, an author asked me how things were going with our attempts to keep "AI" out of the slush pile. It seems like almost no time has passed since I posted an update, but when you are in the thick of things, a sense of time is among the first things to go. In short, it remains a serious problem, the patterns have changed, and we may have to as well. If that's all you wanted to know, you can stop here and go read some more stories.

The good news is that the adaptations we made to our submissions process (documented at neil-clarke.com) are still functioning well enough that we haven't had to close submissions since that initial surge. At its peak, our submissions more than doubled due to the high volume of generated works. Back then, the primary driving force behind those submissions was the side-hustle con-artist communities on YouTube, TikTok, and other venues. They routinely told their audiences that they could generate stories and make easy money by submitting them to people like us, or in several cases, us specifically. While these scams continue to drive traffic, they have stopped growing and have become more erratic/spikey in nature. We can always tell when someone makes a new video and sadly, we've been unable to get any of the hosting platforms to take action. It's likely this type of nonsense will continue in some capacity for the foreseeable future.

If that was the extent of our problems, I'd be happy. Those patterns are predictable and easier to catch. The bad news is that a second group of "AI" users has stepped up to fill a growing portion of that void. These people more closely resemble the patterns of our traditional submitting authors, which means they are more likely to bypass our filter and avoid our attempts to deprioritize generated works in the pool.

In many cases, these works have been "co-written" with "AI" or simply given a polishing edit in an attempt to make them less obvious. While these are more sophisticated attempts to get generated works past us, they still display the hallmarks I've come to expect, and occasionally, they even leave a prompt or ChatGPT response in the text. Given that I've seen some flash and poetry examples of these works find publication elsewhere (the tells are more obvious on longer works), I'd have to rate it as slightly more complicated to recognize. This is one of the few instances I'll admit that there were some advantages to the flood we received.

As this group grows, *and it is growing*, it jeopardizes our ability to properly prioritize human writing and maintain open submissions. That's unacceptable to me.

I was already thinking ahead to this scenario when I wrote my May 2024 editorial on the ethics of using commercial detection tools. Our current process doesn't involve those tools because when we designed and developed it, detection was still heavily flawed. Adding their products would have decreased the accuracy of the pattern-based solution I had developed. The number of false positives and negatives was simply unacceptable and I observed an even greater error rate when it came to works written by non-native English speakers, a group we want to see participating in the process.

When I wrote that editorial, I could see that things were changing. Today, when I observe various hot-takes about detection on social media, I can't help but consider them out of touch and stuck in 2023. If you listen to them, those tools should never be used if even one person is flagged incorrectly.

The truth of the matter is that detection tools will never be 100% accurate. There isn't a person reading this who doesn't rely on a spam filter to manage their email inbox. Those tools have been in development for over thirty years and they still make mistakes. We live with that because the alternative isn't viable. We compensate for its weaknesses by checking our spam filter and pulling back anything we believe it incorrectly classified as spam. That's how "AI" detection should be used and, even without commercial detectors, that's how I'm currently monitoring our submissions. Anything my system deprioritizes as "suspicious" ends up on my desk for a final evaluation. Technology should never have the last word and it won't at *Clarkesworld*.

We should, however, be suspicious of the companies providing detection tools. I've been regularly evaluating these products since 2023 and have found some incredibly dubious vendors. Companies that sell detection *and* detection-avoidance products. Companies that keep the text you submit and don't provide a method for you to opt-out. Companies that use that same text to train LLMs. The list goes on. I previously outlined my own expectations for an ethical detection service:

- Does not use or license works submitted for analysis for training purposes without explicit permission.
- Company is respectful of the rights of creatives in all of their products.
- Accuracy, even with non-native English writers.
- Has an API capable of supporting DOCX and RTF files.
- Affordable for a short fiction publication.
- Does not sell a product that prevents generated text from being detected.

Fortunately, that particular unicorn *does* exist and would be willing to sign a contract that says as much and more. Confidentiality is the highest criteria we should have with regards to submissions and there are actually people who understand that. As they are today, their tools would improve the accuracy of what we've built, even against the rising tide of hybrid or altered text. That may make the difference between staying open or closing, if things continue to get worse.

If any of that makes you nervous, it's not something you need to worry about right now, but you should be thinking about it. We're not at the point where we want to take that leap, but I can see that day coming in the not-so-distant future. How soon depends on how the other side behaves. I'd like to believe that people will come to their senses and stop sending us generated stories or co-writing with something that has produced some of the worst stories I've read. Realistically, I know that won't be the case. That means being prepared and embracing transparency. There are many discussions to have between now and that day.

Let's have that conversation.

ABOUT THE AUTHOR

Neil Clarke is the editor of *Clarkesworld Magazine, Forever Magazine,* and several anthologies, including the Best Science Fiction of the Year series. He is a three-time winner of the Hugo Award for Best Editor Short Form, two-time winner of the Locus Award for Best Editor, a four-time winner of the Chesley Award for Best Art Director, and a recipient of the Kate Wilhelm Solstice Award. His next anthology, *Best Science Fiction of the Year: Volume 8*, was published by Night Shade Books in September. He currently lives in NJ with his wife and two sons.

Blue Ship

COVER ART BY PASCAL BLANCHÉ

ABOUT THE ARTIST

Pascal Blanché is a French artist, with more than twenty-five years of experience in the gaming industry. By day, he works at Behaviour Interactive as Art Director. By night, he likes to work on more personal explorations and build bold new worlds.

Printed in Dunstable, United Kingdom

66863312R00088